DATE DUE

DEC 10 '90		
MAR 23 '93		
SEP 24		
MAY		
OCT 30		
OCT 12		
GAYLORD		PRINTED IN U.S.A.

Star without a Sky

Star without a Sky

Leonie Ossowski

translation by Ruth Crowley

Lerner Publications Company • Minneapolis

Originally published by Beltz & Gelberg under the title *Stern
ohne Himmel.* Copyright © 1978 by Beltz Verlag, Weinheim
und Basel. Programm Beltz & Gelberg, Weinheim.
Translation copyright © 1985 by Lerner Publications Company.

LIBRARY OF CONGRESS CATALOGING IN PUBLICATION DATA

Ossowski, Leonie, 1925-
  Star without a sky.

  Translation of: Stern ohne Himmel.
  Summary: In the last chaotic days of World War II, five
young Germans discover a Jewish boy hiding in a cellar and
are torn over whether or not to turn him over to the Nazi
authorities as the law demands.
  [1. World War, 1939-1945—Germany—Fiction.
2. Jews—Germany—Fiction. 3. Conduct of Life—Fiction]
I. title.

PZ7.0837St   1985   [Fic]   84-21834
ISBN 0-8225-0771-4

Manufactured in the United States of America

1 2 3 4 5 6 7 8 9 10 94 93 92 91 90 89 88 87 86 85

FOREWORD

In April of 1945, when *Star without a Sky* takes place, Hitler and his National Socialist, or Nazi, party had been ruling Germany for twelve years. Under the Nazi regime, Germany had invaded Poland in 1939, initiating World War II. Germany had been at war for over five years when the story opens, and it was clear to any realistic observer that the war was winding down and that Germany had lost. For much of the world, Germany's—and Hitler's—defeat was cause for rejoicing. It would be the end of a terrifying, inhumane regime. For the young people in *Star without a Sky*, however, whose ages range from ten to sixteen, it was the end of the only world they had ever known. Their feelings about the impending German defeat were understandably mixed.

The small town in which the story occurs is east of Berlin, in what is now the German Democratic Republic, more familiarly known as East Germany. The town is a cross-section of German attitudes, hopes, and fears surrounding the defeat. At the time of the story, Germany is being squeezed in a pincer movement by her enemies. U.S. and British troops have entered Germany from the west, and the Russians are marching on Berlin from the east. German refugees are flooding through town from the east to avoid the Russians; there are so many of them that refugee camps have been set up in the towns along the way.

Boys raised under National Socialism were automatically members of the Hitler Youth, an organization designed to instill Nazi values in young children. They were taught to put Germany and its leader, or fatherland and Führer, ahead of individual conscience and human sympathy. They were drilled to obey without question. The Nazis passed laws discriminating against certain groups of people, including Jews. So that they could be clearly identified, all Jews were made to wear a yellow cloth patch in the shape of a star on their clothing. It was the Star of David, which for centuries has symbolized the Jewish faith.

The novel's title, *Star without a Sky*, refers to that star and has other meanings as well. It signifies Abiram and other Jews like him, who were yanked away from their homes and families, put into camps, and often killed. They are the stars and the life they had known is the sky, taken away by the Nazis. Finally, since the German word for sky also means heaven, the title points up one of the author's own beliefs: we make our own world, for better or worse, and cannot look to heaven for help. We are all, in a sense, stars without a sky.

Ossowski included an Afterword in the German edition of this book in which she explains how she happened to write *Star without a Sky*. Shortly after the war, she was sitting with friends in a bombed-out building in East Berlin. One of them told the story of Abiram, which had actually taken place. The group made the man repeat the story again and again, both because it was true and because it gave them hope for the future.

Ossowski wrote *Star without a Sky* over twenty years ago. It was published then in the German Democratic Republic and has been brought out in West Germany recently in order to explain to young people today what it was like to experience Hitler's Germany and the war's end—and to warn against the dangers of blind obedience.

RUTH CROWLEY

1

THE COVERED WAGONS made people uneasy. They had begun passing by weeks ago, with long intervals between each caravan. People stared at them because they were outfitted like gypsy wagons. But as time went by, everyone grew more afraid. Day and night the wheels rolled past on either side of the big boarding-school building and across the market square. The monotonous signals to the horses, the creaking of the wheels, the howling of strange dogs startled the townspeople out of their sleep. Every day there seemed to be less hope that the flight was meant only for other people.

Rumors flew from house to house. People told stories, people exaggerated, people stirred up fear. Handcarts and bicycles were being loaded in backyards and basements, hidden from the neighbors, because it was forbidden to leave without orders.

Mrs. Nagold looked out of the windows of her apartment on the top floor of the boarding school. Up to now she had tried to keep her thoughts about fleeing under control. She had done her duty in the boarding school as a teacher's wife, she had taken care of the boys, she had taken over in the kitchen when one morning the cook had disappeared with bag and baggage. She had tried to believe the optimistic talk of Director Jähde that Adolf Hitler would produce the right weapon at the right moment. But where was that weapon, when the wagons were already coming from a place hardly sixty miles away?

Mrs. Nagold shut her eyes. Slowly, slowly, the horror took hold of her too. She didn't fight it. On the contrary, she seemed relieved to be able to give in to this fear and to act accordingly.

Hurriedly she turned away from the window and began to pack at random. She tore open drawers and closets. She scattered underwear, books, canned goods, and shoes over the table and floor. She filled suitcases, sacks, and bags until it dawned on her that she couldn't carry more than one suitcase.

Since the last air attack the oak door of the boarding school had been jammed, and the woman who had hurried across the square needed both hands to push it open. There was an unaccustomed quiet in the high entryway. Hesitantly she picked up a hairpin that had fallen from her hair as she entered. She looked around and found herself facing a lifesized bust of Adolf Hitler. The woman looked away, ashamed. At the same moment the voices of the choir students filled the whole entryway. Their teacher Nagold had begun choir practice in the auditorium.

The boarding-school students were used to obeying without question, so they kept on singing as the door was yanked open and the mother of the youngest choir student stepped between their rows. Before the teacher had time to give the signal to stop, the woman pressed both hands to her ears and shouted: "Quiet!" Then she reached for a skinny ten-year-old and dragged him forward. "Come on, let's go," she barked at him. The boy resisted. He dug his heels in, his face turned red from the effort and from embarrassment.

"I don't want to," he cried angrily and loud enough for everyone to hear. But his mother pulled him away, and he could see the mockery and contempt in the eyes of his fellow students.

"You can't just burst in on a class like that," Nagold said kindly. "Why don't you wait? The choir practice won't last long today."

"Wait?" the woman shouted scornfully. "Until the Russians come?" Her glance slid over the tall blond man all the way down to his legs, which looked remarkably awkward and unmatched.

"That," she said and pointed to Nagold's artificial leg, "that wasn't enough for you?"

"I don't know," Nagold said more firmly, "whether now is the right time to discuss my amputation."

The woman pulled her son to her. "My Manfred isn't going to wind up in Siberia," she shouted.

The boy knew how silly his mother's words seemed. He had always been the skinniest one in the class, and he imagined he could hear the ringing laughter of the boys as he had seen the scorn in their eyes earlier.

"I don't want to," he cried again. His voice sounded shrill. He stamped his foot.

Without a word Nagold opened the door. He didn't want to expose his students to a mother's hysteria any longer.

Mrs. Steiner dragged Manfred to the door. He stumbled and began to cry.

Nagold waited a while. Then he asked, "Can you imagine Manfred in Siberia?"

The boys shook their heads; a few giggled.

"Fear is more dangerous than the Russians," Nagold continued. His words sounded foolish to him.

"It's more dangerous because it makes people stupid, and in these times we have to be more alert than ever."

"Yes sir, Mr. Nagold," someone called from the rows of choristers.

Nagold was startled. What was that supposed to mean? He peered questioningly into the faces of his students. "Take a break now and we'll practice more this afternoon."

Soon after his wound had healed, Nagold had resumed his post as choir director and music teacher in the school. He had entered the war a healthy, whole man and had returned a cripple. His former colleague Jähde had meanwhile taken over the office of principal. Even in prewar times Jähde had been known and feared as a strict proponent of National Socialism. Thus he never let an opportunity pass to call in the boys' choir for Party proclamations and celebrations.

While Nagold had been fighting at the front, was wounded and lost a leg, Jähde had been promoted. The brand-new principal had jovially clapped him on the shoulder at his reinstatement and said, "Chin up, Nagold, even though you can't fight for Führer and fatherland at the front, there are still things to be done here. We need people like you. Help me turn this children's song club, with all its false tradition, into a German youth choir that our Führer and our city can be proud of."

Jähde had extended his hand to shake Nagold's, but Nagold had ignored it. Since that day there had been unacknowledged hostility between the two men.

Thus Nagold, without knowing it, had become one of the prime adversaries of the principal, who was determined to do away with these church hymns his music teacher cultivated.

But the last few weeks had frustrated Mr. Jähde's plans for the future as well. It was impossible to run the school as usual, since most of the older students had been drafted into the Home Guard. All the teachers except Jähde and Nagold were at the front. Still, the choir continued. Jähde even insisted on keeping up the weekly singing of vespers. But in fact, in keeping the school going he was struggling to save his own skin, since only as a school principal was he exempt from military service.

Nagold had no idea of his wife's sudden plans to flee. Some days ago he had sharply dismissed this possibility, especially since there were now several children in the school who had lost contact with their parents because of the rapid advance of the Soviet troops. His wife's moaning about the loss of their possessions and her miserable fear of personal danger had provoked him to unusual harshness. It had been the first overt argument of their marriage.

When Nagold was confronted with the chaos in his apartment, he could hardly control himself at first. He brushed a pile of underwear from the chair and sat down.

"What are you doing?"

"I'm packing, like everyone else!"

"Who else?"

Mrs. Nagold didn't answer but kept on packing while he watched her. The silence between them became unbearable. She would have liked to run to him and beg him to help pack, to come along, not to leave her alone with this horrible fear. Instead she held out two sweaters to him.

"Do you want to take both of them or just the patterned one?" she said, and tried to make her words sound natural. "That one may be enough, two take up too much room. We could take your music instead, or . . ."

He just looked at her. Her voice was trembling. Slowly she lowered her hands. Her eyes filled with tears.

Silently Nagold began to clean up. He picked things up at random and put them back in their old places. "You're packing suitcases," he said quietly. "A hysterical woman pulls her ten-year-old child out of school because she imagines him in the Siberian mines. And I'm supposed to sing with the boys." He watched with sympathy as she cried quietly. Her eyelids were swollen, and red patches stood out on her broad cheekbones.

She didn't abandon the hope that naked fear might suddenly grab him too and drive him to her side.

"Do you want to stay here when the Russians come? Do you want to watch them take us all away? Beat the children and—" her voice sank to a whisper, "rape the women? Maybe me?"

Nagold pounded the table with his fist.

"Do you think they wouldn't catch us if I take off with my wooden leg and a suitcase in my hand?"

The idea of galloping along in front of Russian tanks with an artificial leg and two suitcases amused him. He began to laugh and kept laughing heartily until he noticed the horror in her eyes.

"You're laughing?"

"Yes," he said with irritation, "sometimes you just laugh, even when it's not funny."

She didn't know what to answer and felt disappointed. Hadn't she been thinking about him as well as herself? Was the desire for security so absurd?

It seemed as if he had read her thoughts.

"And what about the boys? Have you forgotten about them? They've been entrusted to us, after all. That's a responsibility we've both taken on. You, too."

He didn't wait for an answer. He went over to her and lifted her chin.

"Stop your packing."

She nodded obediently.

"Yes, of course, the boys," she murmured and looked up at him. Mechanically he stroked her hair a few times. It did her good, and she tried to smile. "We're all a little confused," he said and was relieved that she had noticed nothing of his loneliness.

2

IT HAD BECOME part of the daily routine for refugees to share meals with the townspeople. This was the practice all over town, because the public soup kitchens were no longer large enough to accommodate the number of people passing through.

Director Jähde wanted to feed as many refugees as possible at the boarding school. He thought that he had to set a good example. He sat self-importantly at the head of the table between his students and the Nagolds. His lively eyes watched the refugees distrustfully. He didn't like the quiet, hungry way they spooned in food. Its very naturalness seemed a reproach to him.

Usually he couldn't bear the silence for long. He would ask about the German troops and be told instead about the Russian advances. Every time that happened, it was the impetus for him to repeat the comforting news from the official bulletins. The strangers would nod their heads, and some of them would venture an impertinent comment. The boys seldom took part in these conversations; they often didn't even listen. The education and protection the adult realm usually offered them, the price of which was obedience, seemed increasingly dubious to them in the last few days. They had their own thoughts and plans.

The largest of the boys was named Antek. Despite his sixteen years, Jähde had gotten him an exemption from the Home Guard because his voice in the choir was irreplaceable. When the other members of his class proudly entered the war to defend the fatherland, women, and children, Antek thought he would never recover from the shame that his contribution to final victory was to be limited to singing. He had gone to the principal, he had begged and pleaded with Nagold as an old soldier for understanding, and finally he had demanded help from his Hitler Youth leader. But all his efforts were in vain. Director Jähde had curtly turned him away. The patriotic feelings of the sixteen-year-old had made little impression on him. Nagold, on the other hand, had had more time for his student. He had taken him up to his apartment, had sat down behind his desk and let Antek talk.

Antek had pointed out to Nagold the duties of youth under National Socialism. And those duties were not singing, but fighting, in order to bring all-out war to final victory, even at the cost of one's life. His teacher's patient attention had pleased Antek; he thought he had won.

"You tell me yourself, Mr. Nagold, isn't it more important for a boy of sixteen and a half to go to the front than to sing in church?"

Nagold had stood up, and it had seemed to Antek that his wooden leg stamped twice as loudly as usual over the floorboards.

17

"If there were any point to it, Antek, I would agree with you that it's better to fight than to sing cantatas. But the war has become senseless for us. If you can't believe in victory, you're not fighting honestly anymore."

At first Antek hadn't grasped Nagold's words at all. He had never before heard anyone say so clearly that the war was lost for Germany. You weren't even allowed to think something like that.

"But," he had stuttered, "if that were true, and it's certainly not, not as long as there's a single German soldier—"

"Have you ever seen a Russian soldier or an American or a French or an English soldier?" Nagold had barked at him.

Antek had been shocked and had shaken his head.

"Then don't talk such damned nonsense."

"But then what's going to become of us?"

Nagold had nodded as if he had posed this question to himself a thousand times, had shrugged his shoulders as he often did, looked at Antek and said, "Nothing."

"Nothing?" Antek had whispered, "how can you say that?"

"Well, you're going to have to get used to it, because in a few weeks or a few days everybody will be saying it, not just me. Then it will be all over. Then there won't be any more fatherland to fight for."

Antek had jumped up. A wild anger had smothered any answer in him. He had run out of the room without speaking and had had to rein himself in to keep from slamming the door after him.

From that day on Antek's love for his teacher had changed to contempt. He avoided Nagold's company.

From that time on Nagold was a coward in Antek's eyes, a man without patriotism, a teacher who didn't deserve the trust of his students.

Antek had then gone to his Hitler Youth leader, who had immediately promised to do what he could for him. But even these efforts failed, due to the close relationship between Director Jähde and the district leader of the Hitler Youth. And that had sealed Antek's fate. He was not allowed to become a soldier.

At night he would lie awake for a long time and when he finally fell asleep, he would be plagued by nightmares. In class Antek became inattentive, answered back, and surprised his schoolmates with his unaccustomed rebelliousness toward the adults. He became sullen and rude to his friends.

Antek's thoughts were interrupted abruptly. Paule poked him.

"Look at her over there," he said and pointed unobtrusively to a pregnant woman who was greedily slurping her watery soup. "Look how hungry she is." Paule leaned closer to his friend. "We can make a deal with her for sure. Ask what she'll give for seconds."

Antek stirred his soup without eating. It would be the right thing to be like Paule, he thought, to worry about nothing but taking care of your own needs as quietly and safely as possible. Without a word, Antek shoved his soup over to the woman. "Take it," he said.

"You idiot!" Paule hissed, enraged. Antek had botched his deal. After all, the soup had to be sold while it was still warm.

He kicked the boy sitting opposite on the shin. "Soup?" The boy nodded.

"What'll you pay?"

"I don't have anything."

Paule took his soup plate back and drew his spoon through his lips, smacking them. The boy swallowed hard. Paule feverishly thought what he could get out of the boy. Everybody had some kind of treasure, and then Paule saw the boy's.

"Your alarm whistle," he hissed.

The boy shoved his precious whistle across the table. But Antek was quicker than Paule. He snatched the whistle out of the boy's hand and pocketed it.

"Get it back from me later."

Then he turned to Paule. "Either give him your soup for nothing or you don't come with us afterwards. It's up to you."

Antek had a real desire to spoil his friend's deal. But it wasn't the first time that food had been traded for other things. Antek had seen it happen daily and not objected. Today was different. Paule pushed his soup across the table without getting anything for it. In a muffled rage he sat brooding on how to get even with Antek. Nobody could push Paule around like that, and he had no intention of doing without anything. Antek was the strongest, Antek had the key to the door of their storeroom, so it was up to Antek whether you had to toss down a watery cabbage soup out of necessity or whether you sold it because you could fill up on better food. Paule looked longingly at Willi and Zick, who were cheerfully selling their soup as usual.

"You'll pay for that, Antek," Paule said slowly.

Antek didn't deign to look at his friend. "Is that a threat?"

"I don't care what you call it, but nobody gets away with doing that to Paule." Whenever Paule was angry he referred to himself by his first name.

"It's ridiculous, the fuss you're making about some watery soup."

Paule wheeled around. His triangular face got even paler, only his ears turned red with anger.

"Watery soup?" He leaned over to Antek. "You mean alarm whistle."

Antek shook his head. "No," he said calmly, "I mean watery soup."

"You've botched a deal for Paule and you'll pay for that. I swear it."

Antek didn't take that seriously. He shrugged, bored, and tossed out a scornful "How?"

Director Jähde gave the signal to rise. That was the beginning of the free time the boys had been waiting for. Antek, Paule, Willi, and Zick listened impatiently to Nagold's warnings to be back promptly at three for practice.

3

WHILE WILLI AND ZICK waited for Antek in front of the building, Paule had already gone on ahead. He hadn't wanted to walk over with Antek. He needed time to figure out how best to get his revenge.

"Are you hungry too?" Zick asked plaintively.

Willi looked at the smaller boy with contempt. "You can never control yourself, it's always the same thing."

"People can't help being hungry," Zick answered angrily. "My stomach isn't even a stomach anymore, it's just a hole as big as your rear end."

"I'm not going to answer that," said Willi, furious.

"No, because you're hungry too. You're just too fat, it doesn't show. But with me . . ."

As if to illustrate what he was saying, he bent over double and perched on the stone steps.

"If you were any older than ten, I'd beat you up, but I don't hurt children."

Willi doubled up his belt and paced arrogantly up and down. Finally Antek came.

"I'm just going to get Ruth," he called to the other two. "Do you want to come along?" Zick and Willi didn't want to.

"That girl is always along," Willi complained, "we've been waiting long enough."

"At least give us the key," Zick suggested. Antek hesitated. "Where's Paule?"

"We don't know. He'll be along."

"Okay." Antek tossed the key to Willi and disappeared in the direction of the granary.

Zick and Willi laughed. As if on a raid, the two of them slipped through the wagons standing across the square. The street that ran on this side of the square led to the city wall as far as the old gate, behind which the new section of town lay. It had been destroyed and burnt down to the foundations and offered a picture of desolation. Water had collected in craters a yard deep. It smelled of putrefaction, and rats crouched beside the slimy puddles. Among the garbage and the rot, in the midst of stench and death, they lived undisturbed. Willi and Zick clambered through the ruins.

"Here's Schiller Street," said Willi and turned left.

The path became narrower and narrower. They had almost reached the end of the bombed-out section. The quiet was uncanny.

"Would you like to walk along here at night?" asked Zick.

Willi nearly said no. But he got control of himself. "Of course, if it were an order."

Zick thought about Willi's words. "Do you think what we're doing is right?"

Willi stood still. "Right!" he exclaimed in astonishment. "What does that mean?" He pointed with both arms from the town wall along stones, ruins, craters, to the fields outside town. "After all, everybody here is dead, right?"

He said it with indifference and as naturally as if it were an everyday thing for a few hundred people to be killed by bombs. It probably was natural as far as he was concerned. He didn't know anything else.

"And if you were dead?"

Willi's fat face laughed.

"Well, I'm not, and if you keep on asking such stupid questions I'll beat you up."

After a pause he added seriously, "Maybe I'll die—as a soldier or as a member of the Hitler Youth, fighting for the Führer."

Openmouthed, Zick looked at his friend. Willi became friendlier.

"But first I'd fight, defend us. With my bare hands, if I had to. I won't run away like the refugees or Manfred today at practice. I tell you, Zick, I'll get those Russian pigs with grenades, like this." Willi took a piece of pipe that was lying on the ground, crouched down, aimed at an invisible tank, got ready to leap, flung the pipe into the air and cried: "For Führer and fatherland!"

The pipe splashed into one of the bomb craters filled with water.

"You idiot, that was pure copper!"

Willi and Zick turned around. Paule was standing behind them.

"I'm collecting copper and you blockhead, you throw it into the water—as a grenade! That's so stupid!"

Paule slid down the hill and pulled the pipe out of the mire. "Grenade," he grunted again and shook his head, "that's worth money, not for Führer and fatherland, but for Paule!"

Willi was obviously upset. He wanted to change the subject as quickly as possible, so he pulled the key out of his pocket and let it dangle slowly.

"Man, you've got the key!" Paule said.

His eyes gleamed with the promise that represented.

"Yeah, I've got the key," Willi aped.

Paule put his pipe down with the others. "I have an idea," he said. All three squatted down on the ground.

At the very beginning of Market Street stood one of the oldest buildings in the city. The sun hit the tiny windows only in the early morning. The beams had been full of dry rot for years. Moss had eaten its way under the roof shingles so that the damp reached down to the stairs, and in the entryway there was always a smell of mold and damp wood. Even before the war, the housing authorities had wanted to close down the building.

The former principal, Kimmich, had been held in preventive custody for a year because he was politically suspect. When he was released from the camp, he returned to his home town. On the spot he was given the old house with two rooms and a kitchen. All the other rooms had been made uninhabitable by bombings.

Kimmich had no choice but to accept it. Nagold, out of a certain affection, had seen to it that he was able to earn a little money as a music copyist. So Kimmich lived like a hermit with his fourteen-year-old grand-daughter Ruth, avoided by one part of the townspeople and forgotten by the rest. He was forbidden to pursue his profession or to perform his compositions.

Antek crept along the side of the granary until he was in Ruth's range of hearing. Then he lifted his hands to his mouth and imitated a screech-owl at short intervals. Antek saw the crooked door with the iron knocker shoved open and then Ruth appeared.

He turned around and sauntered off in the same direction as Willi and Zick. Only when he thought he was completely safe from the teachers and Kimmich did he stop.

"Did your grandfather notice anything?" he asked. As always when she was there, he didn't know how to behave at first. He was embarrassed. His question seemed unnecessary to him. Ruth shook her head.

"Well, come on, the others are waiting."

For a while they walked along without talking. When their hands brushed against each other or he helped her in climbing over the piles of rubbish, he felt her glance.

Antek walked ahead.

"Look, the sun," said Ruth.

Antek didn't answer. Girls sometimes said the most obvious things and thought they were discovering one of the wonders of the world.

"Down here," he heard her say, "it's like walking in a trench."

"How do you know what it's like to walk in a trench!"

"I don't know any more about it than you, or have you maybe seen one?"

"No, not yet," said Antek, "but I'll manage it, you can bet on it."

Ruth felt that her words had hurt him. She was sorry.

"Antek." She pulled on his sleeve until he stopped. "Would you still like to be a soldier?" she asked softly.

"Would I like to? It's not a question of my liking to. I have to become a soldier, and I also intend to. If we lose the war, it's all over. Then there's no more fatherland and no more faith, and nothing makes sense anymore."

Antek had echoed Nagold without realizing it, except

26

that in his words there was nothing of resignation; there was deep despair.

"I don't know," said Ruth. Now she was walking ahead because she thought that Antek would become angry again at her words. "Grandfather always says that when the war is over," her steps became quicker, "and if we lose, then our life will really start."

Cautiously she turned her head to look at him. She had never before told anyone her grandfather's opinions. She was old enough to know what kind of danger that could mean for him. Her anxious glance met Antek's fixed stare.

"What did your grandfather say?" he asked hoarsely. She couldn't tell at first whether anger or astonishment had choked off his voice.

But she didn't have time to answer. A screech-owl's cry sounded close by. Seconds later Zick landed in a ball at their feet, surrounded by a cloud of dust.

"Where have you been?" he asked, acting as if it were his distinctive style to get around in this way.

"Did you hurt yourself?" Ruth looked with concern at Zick's scraped knee. He must have slipped and fallen from the wall.

He shook his head. "No, why should I have? I just took a shortcut." Zick liked to play at being a brave man when Ruth was around.

"Well, then it's a good thing that you found us so fast," smiled Antek.

When Paule had sent Zick off with the excuse that he should look for the others, Willi became impatient.

"What are you doing?" he asked. "Antek said he would bring Ruth here."

Paule motioned him to be quiet. "I know. But I

wanted to be alone with you." He stuck his hands in his pockets and looked at Willi out of the corner of his eye.

"Now you have the key."

Willi nodded.

"Don't you want to keep it?"

"Why should I?"

"Well, you're fifteen, the second-oldest of us!"

"You're fifteen too."

"But I'm two months younger than you. If someone's going to keep it, we should go in order."

Willi was flattered. He wasn't used to this kind of modesty from Paule.

"What does it matter whether or not I have the key?"

Paule squinted still more. "For instance, then it's up to you whether and when we come here."

Slowly Willi began to find this appealing. "Not a bad idea!"

"Okay, then let's say after a week it's my turn, then Ruth."

"No, not her!" Willi interrupted. "I'm not going to let some kid whose grandfather was a political prisoner tell me when I can eat."

Paule laughed. "Just wait, maybe she'll turn out to be a good connection yet."

Willi didn't know what Paule meant.

"If I have the key she doesn't get to come along!"

"Give it to me."

Paule watched his friend closely. Now he would find out whether his carefully laid plan would work. Paule knew for certain that if this maneuver failed, he would never get his hands on the key.

Willi was too preoccupied with playing boss to notice any underhandedness in Paule. He held the key out.

"It's nothing special just to look at. But what you can open with it . . ." He clicked his tongue suggestively.

Paule grabbed for the key and stuck it in his pocket.

"What are you doing?"

"Nothing, nothing at all," Paule answered in a friendly way and returned the key. Willi had no idea that Paule's agile fingers had pressed the key against a piece of wax in his pocket and had made an impression of it.

What had once been Schiller Street was now only ruins. Despite all the destruction, a few walls had remained upright. A picture of the Alps, hanging at an angle with a broken frame on the wall of a second-story room, looked melancholy and ridiculous at the same time. In one corner dangled a dented stovepipe.

The children didn't look up. Antek felt that Paule and Willi had ganged up on him. Paule had made good his threat and turned Willi against him. All because of that boy's ridiculous alarm whistle. As if there weren't more important problems to worry about. But he had no desire to start a fistfight, especially with both of them against him. Zick was no help. Anyway, you never knew which side he would take.

"As far as I'm concerned," Antek said in irritation, "Willi can keep the key. Do what you want."

Paule grinned.

"If Ruth comes along, I won't open up," said Willi. Antek had begun to move the boards aside. At Willi's words he straightened up, jumped Willi from behind, and twisted his arm behind his back until Willi fell to his knees.

"Enough for you?" Antek asked and jerked Willi's wrist higher.

29

Willi could only groan and nod. Antek let him go. None of the boys had looked at Ruth, who had stood by waiting and was now silently clearing away the boards as if nothing had happened.

An iron cellar door became visible behind a broken pillar lodged in a cement block. It was always hard work to shove the hunk of cement far enough aside that the door could be opened, but this trouble was necessary in order to hide the entrance. The boys grabbed hold of the block. Zick gave the order. Willi's face grew red from exertion. Paule helped with an iron bar, and Antek steadied the pillar so that it didn't slide too far.

"Watch out," said Paule as he tossed the iron bar aside. They were finished.

"Who has the candle?"

Ruth gave it up reluctantly. "It's so dark down there," she complained.

"Exactly," said Willi and pushed the iron bolt back.

Darkness and the smell of damp masonry rushed toward them. One by one they climbed down the half-buried cellar stairs, which ended in a long corridor. Something scurried past Ruth.

"Rats," said Paule.

Ruth held on to Antek's jacket until he gave her his hand comfortingly. The candle gave just enough light for Willi to find his way. As the last one, Zick had to feel his way through the dark. No one spoke, the shadows played on the wall, and somewhere they heard water dripping. All five were anxious to reach their goal.

Then Zick screamed. Something had ambushed him from behind and was holding onto his sweater with an iron grip. The children, pursued by Zick's cries, ran ahead. At the end of the corridor, where a little gray daylight was visible, they stopped. Zick had fallen silent. Antek took the candle from Willi and dove once more into the ominous darkness of the cellar. He carried the candle high and held his arm as if he were expecting an attack.

"It was just a nail," a small voice suddenly announced, and then Zick was illuminated by the candlelight. He pointed to a hole in his sweater. As proof he held out to Antek a rusty nail on which he seemed to have been snagged.

"Idiot," hissed Antek. He pushed Zick roughly along in front of him.

Willi wiped the sweat from his forehead.

"Next time you can stay hooked on the nail, you scaredy-cat!" he said. "Or you can go get him for a change," Antek interrupted.

Ruth laughed.

"Oh, no, not that," Paule groaned. "He'll lose his appetite."

Appetite—they forgot their quarrel. After all, they hadn't come here to show how brave they were. They had come because they were hungry and because they wanted to eat in peace. Willi busied himself with a wooden door that gave access to a wooden bin. With a broad gesture he flung the door open.

Sausage, jam, preserves, raisins, ham, raspberry juice, sugar cubes, pickles!

Willi stood in front of a shelf with his eyes closed. In his mind he let all the pleasurable tastes slide over his tongue, then reached for a hard sausage that smelled wonderful. Zick scurried here and there. As he was stuffing his mouth with raisins he was overcome with a desire for ham, and as soon as he had the ham in his

31

mouth he felt he had to have sauerkraut immediately. He ate and ate until he became sick and vomited through a hole in the wall of the corridor.

Paule, on the other hand, was very systematic. He surveyed the provisions, composed a menu for himself, and carefully carried what he had chosen to his seat. Today he was eating liverwurst on slices of ham, peaches with zwieback toast, and almonds and raisins for dessert. He was drinking a bottle of black currant juice.

Antek had opened a jar of cherries. He held it out to Ruth. "These are your favorite, aren't they?"

He first saw to it that Ruth got what she wanted. Only then did he begin his own meal.

Now all five of them were sitting on crates, shelves, and baskets. They were eating and drinking and laughing and were proud to have what the adults had to do without. Antek thought no more about the starving woman to whom he had given a plate of cabbage soup an hour ago. Paule had long since forgotten the alarm whistle, and Willi no longer cared whether Ruth was allowed to eat her fill too.

Ruth had often tried to take along something for her grandfather. But her friends had become angry. Although none of them except Willi had anything against old Kimmich, they didn't want to allow her to take food to him. The more people who knew about it, the greater the danger of losing their treasure and of going hungry.

Paule was the one who suddenly noticed a noise among all the chewing and smacking of lips.

"Be quiet for a minute!"

Now they all heard it, shuffling, light tapping, in between silence.

"Oh, it's just the nail again," Willi said to give himself courage, but his eyes glittered and his lips got dry. Zick squeezed the ham between his fingers until the fat ran. Paule stood ready to leap, a full jar of preserves in his hand.

"Come on, hide!" whispered Antek.

He pushed Ruth behind some sacks. Zick sprang after her. Willi squeezed himself into a crate of potatoes and Paule found a hiding place in an upright zinc tub standing near the door. In seconds it was as quiet as a tomb. The cans and jars lay abandoned on the floor as five pairs of eyes stared through slits, from behind baskets, past sausages and jars of food, at the door.

Slowly the wooden door opened. From the darkness of the corridor emerged a boy. He must have been barely older than Paule. His pitiable thinness made an uncanny impression on the children. They watched, horrified, as he knelt on the floor and pulled down jars and containers. He didn't even use the spoon that was lying in front of him. He plunged his hands into the liverwurst and smeared it into his mouth, then the plum jam and so on, whatever he came across.

As always, Zick had eaten too much. Now, when he was forced to watch this intruder stuff handfuls of liverwurst into his mouth, he got thoroughly sick. He belched loudly.

The stranger, shocked, jumped up. He hesitated only a moment, then he grabbed the sausage Willi had bitten into and scurried toward the door. Suddenly, as if he had sprung up out of the earth, there stood Paule. He threw himself on the skinny boy who stumbled against the zinc tub, almost senseless with terror. With a tinny rumble it fell over on both boys.

Willi scrambled out of his potato crate and yelled, "A thief! A thief!" He had forgotten completely that they themselves were nothing but thieves.

He pushed the tub upright again and pulled the stranger out by the legs. Paule, made bolder by Willi's help, rolled the enemy over onto his back and knelt on his upper arm.

"Search him!" he coughed.

Willi fumbled around in the shabby rags.

"Why did he have to interfere with us?" Antek grumbled. He was uncomfortable with the situation, but he didn't want to stop his friends. It was bad enough that they had been surprised here.

4

WILLI HAD FOUND SOMETHING. It wasn't much, just a scrap of material; angry that he hadn't found any loot, he threw it aside. Then the stranger rebelled. He kicked his legs, he even tried to bite Paule, and wild rage was in his black eyes.

"You louse, I'll teach you to try that with me," Paule said and rammed his leg harder against the boy's arm.

"Let's have a look at that rag," Antek suggested.

Zick lifted the piece of material with two fingers. They all stared at the rag, on which a Jewish star was sewn. Willi and Paule let the stranger go. None of them had actually ever seen a star of David, since Jews didn't exist but were just something people complained about. As they passed the rag around in amazement, the boy thought he saw a chance to escape. Without looking around, Paule reached behind himself and snagged him.

"You'd like that, wouldn't you?" He shoved the boy against the wall, where he slumped, exhausted and discouraged. Now he didn't care what happened, let them do what they wanted with him. He couldn't defend himself anymore, couldn't think anymore, couldn't eat anymore.

Willi strode over to him. "Where did you get the Jewish star?"

The boy wasn't listening. He looked into Willi's red face and thought: When you're dead, you won't be so fat anymore, and flies will walk across your eyes, just like . . .

Antek shoved Willi aside.

"Stop it, can't you see he's had it?"

"How did you get the Jewish star?"

Antek got no answer. He didn't really need one, since he knew perfectly well that no one in Germany carried that star around of his own free will. He was looking at a Jew. Uncut curls hung down at the sides of his face. His high-arched brows could have been drawn with charcoal, and the famous Jewish nose was hardly hooked but very narrow.

"Are you a Jew?" Antek asked.

"Yes."

The others drew back.

The word "Jew" raised a wall of contempt around the stranger. He closed his eyes.

"Man, a Jew." Zick was the first to speak, still very distressed at this monstrous occurrence. Then curiosity got the better of him. Cautiously he touched the boy.

Antek pushed him away. The crippling silence of his friends occupied his thoughts. What should I do with him, kept hammering through his mind. What do Paule and Willi think? Why don't they say anything? With rage he felt the responsibility that his friends were forcing on him.

"Why don't you say something?" he snarled at Willi. "A few minutes ago you wanted to be boss and kept the key!"

Willi just looked sheepish.

Paule was standing in the corner. It was best not to get involved in something like this too soon. Zick was staring openmouthed.

"Oh, what business is it of mine," growled Antek in his frustration and threw an apple against the wall.

The Jew winced.

Ruth had been frightened too. At first it had looked as if Antek wanted to throw the apple at the stranger. Ruth jumped up. Antek went over to Paule and Willi, shoved some cans aside and said, "This is really a mess."

Paule and Willi nodded.

No one would look at the stranger.

"Ask him his name," Antek heard Ruth say, "and where he's going."

Why was she shouting so? But Ruth hadn't shouted. She had just come closer and closer to him. He turned around. He looked into her green eyes and saw her scorn at his cowardice. Maybe he would have behaved differently if Paule and Willi hadn't been there, but how could he explain that to her now?

"Don't let her fool with you," Willi broke in.

It sounded cutting, as if a threat might follow. But Willi didn't make one. Antek had understood. Ruth turned away. All her movements expressed deep contempt.

"Tell us, what's your name?" she asked the boy.

Antek rushed out of his corner and pulled the girl back roughly. He felt that he was hurting her. "Don't you talk to him. This is none of your business. This is our concern."

Without answering Antek, she rubbed her arm where he had grabbed her. He's jealous, she thought. Willi's unspoken threat had made little impression on her, so the cowardice of her friend pained her all the more.

"You only think about yourself!" she flung at him contemptuously and turned again to the Jew.

"Tell me your name or what I should call you," Antek heard her ask confidingly.

The stranger stared into her face.

"Abiram," he said.

"That's a crazy name," Paule remarked in the background. The stranger had forgotten for a moment that he wasn't alone with the girl. He saw the lifted heads of the boys behind her and felt their hostility.

Ruth didn't leave his side.

"Why did you come here?" Willi asked.

Abiram kept his gaze on Ruth. He wanted to answer only her.

"I'm looking for someone," he admitted hesitantly.

That caught Paule's attention. "Here, in this cellar?"

"I don't exactly know, but on this street."

"Everybody's dead here," Antek said drily, "you don't need to keep on looking."

Abiram was tired. Why were they asking him these questions? They would turn him in and take him to a camp. Only the girl was different.

"Okay," Paule interrupted his train of thought, "why are you spying around in our cellar?"

"I wasn't spying, I wanted a place to hide. I'm a Jew."

There was that word again, and again the answer was silence. There was nothing else to say. Curiosity was turning into suspicion and aversion.

Willi thought he had been patient with the stranger long enough. He motioned his friends to come over to the door. They had to make some decisions now.

Ruth stood between the Jew and the friends, and neither the one nor the other talked to her. Abiram still slumped apathetically against the wall. Antek refused to look at Ruth. The group of boys had excluded her. Even Zick paid her no attention. She shoved a jar of stewed fruit over to Abiram with her foot.

"Eat that," she said. She kept looking at Antek. Abiram didn't touch the jar.

"You're probably sorry now," he asked in a whisper and gestured with his head at the boys.

"Nonsense," she answered.

"There's nothing more you can do for me!"

"Just wait!"

Willi looked over to them. "Why are you whispering? Jews have to be turned in, you all know that," he said loudly.

The idea of turning in a half-starved Jew seemed ridiculous to Antek. "You're getting on my nerves, Willi," he said dismissively. "I don't know what to do with a Jew either," he said softly, so that Abiram couldn't hear, "but after all, he's our age."

"So?" Willi objected. "Is that my fault?"

Zick, who was only listening, wondered how it would be if he were the one crouching against the wall there, if he were the one somebody wanted to turn in. The thought made him hot and uncomfortable and he was suddenly very thankful that God had made his father a soldier instead of a Jew.

"I tell you," Willi continued, "the Jew has to go. I'll turn him in."

"Of course it'll be you," said Ruth. "None of the rest of us would do it."

Willi didn't know at first whether that was said with

39

scorn or admiration. "I didn't ask you," he said.

"That's all garbage," Paule said and lowered his voice. "If we turn him in, then the first thing he'll do is betray us. Then everyone will find out about our pantry here." He made an expansive gesture. The five looked at each other. Paule was right, that was a serious danger. Ruth smiled at Antek, but he ignored her. Let her sit down with her Jew again and comfort him, he thought.

The muffled sound of church bells reached the cellar. Zick's eyes widened and became round. "Choir practice . . ."

Practice must have started half an hour ago.

"The Jew stays here!" Paule decided.

"In the pantry?" asked Zick.

"It's the only place we can lock up."

Ruth hesitated. "Then I'll stay here too."

But Antek had taken her arm and was pulling her along.

"You'd like that, wouldn't you!" He pushed her out into the corridor.

The boys followed.

"And don't eat too much, I've counted everything," Paule warned.

Abiram didn't listen. He tried to push his way through. But Willi had figured on that. He hit Abiram, who tumbled backwards. The door fell shut, the key was turned, the Jew was captured.

"I have the key," Willi grinned and kept it carefully in his hand, "and I won't give it up until you're where you belong!"

Abiram didn't make a sound. He wrapped his arms around the slats. He could no longer see Ruth. Paule

40

and Zick disappeared in the darkness. Only Willi gloated over his captive for one proud moment.

"Come on, Willi!" Antek cried.

"Let's get moving!"

Antek looked at Abiram. "We'll be back this evening. Nothing will happen to you." He sensed Abiram's fear. "He's just showing off!" And with that Antek too disappeared in the darkness.

Abiram was alone. He shook the slats. He pounded against the latch. All his exhaustion and weakness had left him. He was obsessed with the thought that no human being would ever come into the cellar again.

"Open up, open up," he called. His voice broke. Then he saw Paule's angry face through the window with the bent bars.

"Don't yell so loud or you'll have the police on your neck before you know it."

Abiram fell silent immediately. But in reality he had nothing to fear. No one ever came by there.

"Don't you feel sorry for him?" asked Ruth, holding Antek back.

"Of course, but that doesn't do any good. Nothing will happen to him for the moment."

"Why did you let them lock him up?"

Antek was impatient. "Because we have practice. We have to figure out what to do with him."

"Is your practice more important? Would you like to be locked up down there?"

"Can I help it," Antek shouted in genuine rage, "if he's a Jew and Willi's a red-hot Hitler Youth member?"

Ruth turned away without a word and took another route home. Antek had to hurry to catch his friends who were stumbling over the ruins. They jumped over ditches and bomb craters, but they couldn't make up the lost time.

"What shall we tell Nagold?" Paule coughed.

"Nothing!"

"Why not the truth?" Willi suggested.

"If you want to earn the German Cross in gold with daggers and clusters presented by Adolf himself, okay, but not at Paule's expense. I'm not going to eat watery soup because of your patriotism, you . . . " Paule shook his copper pipe threateningly in Willi's face.

"I have a stitch in my side," gasped Zick.

"Oh come on," Antek pulled him forward, "you're just afraid. Either you're in this or you're not. No chickening out now."

They wiped the sweat from their faces and stamped the pale dust of the ruins from their shoes.

"What on earth are we going to tell Nagold?" Zick wailed again.

No one answered him. So he trotted along behind his friends, across the street, between the wagons and the refugees, and was sure that everyone could tell by looking at them that they had a Jew stashed in the cellar.

Nagold had waited impatiently. It had never yet happened that his students had been half an hour late coming back from their recess. None of the other children could give him an idea what had happened. One of them had seen Antek running across the market square just after lunch. That was all. Without the four boys a practice was pointless, because he needed every voice. Paule, moreover, had a solo.

Nagold paced up and down in the auditorium. What

could it mean? Was it disobedience on Antek's part, who had been angry and defiant since their conversation? Had something happened to the children? Nagold interrupted his pacing. What if Jähde should come in now and demand an explanation of where the boys are? Nagold put one of the children in charge of the class and left the room.

The windows on the landing at the head of the stairs overlooked the market. Nagold leaned out and saw Zick, the last of the boys, turning the corner. Nagold breathed a sigh of relief. Only now did he notice the stabbing pain in the stump of his leg. His constant pacing had stressed it. Nagold looked over the stair rail and saw the four boys sneaking in. They were running on tiptoe and whispering to each other.

Nagold leaned on the railing to take weight off his leg. Wasn't it madness to stand here in order to punish four children for coming late to class when their fathers were dying a few miles away? Zick was the first one to the stairs. Nagold was hidden by a pillar so that the children thought they were the only ones in the stairwell.

"I just hope Jähde doesn't catch us," Zick whispered.

Nagold had to smile. His fear of Jähde was hardly less than the children's.

"Where have you been?" It didn't even sound harsh.

The boys jumped in surprise. Zick slid back to the last place in the line of friends. No one answered Nagold. Silently they stood on the bottom steps and made not the slightest move to come up. They looked at Nagold in embarrassment as he waited for one of them to give him an explanation. His wooden leg stood at an awkward angle to his healthy one, as always when he was in great pain. "You're half an hour late," he said with agonizing calm.

"Yes," Antek responded. The other boys were glad for anyone to say anything. They nodded and ducked their heads like beaten dogs. Nagold's calmness intensified their perplexity. They knew, of course, that it wasn't his way to use anger or threats, but in this case they would have preferred a concrete bawling-out.

But Nagold was demanding an explanation, he even seemed to be willing to be friendly and understanding. Then too, he was suffering physically. All four boys had seen that immediately.

"Paule," his voice demanded.

Paule looked down and said nothing.

"Zick?"

The little boy's face grew red. His hands became damp and he wiped them several times on the seat of his pants. He didn't say a word.

If the boys had known how tired Nagold was and how thankfully he might have taken any lie as the simple truth, they would probably have come up with an excuse more easily. But as it was, their guilty conscience about the secret of the forbidden pantry made it impossible for them to think at all.

Nagold looked at Willi next. "Well?" he asked.

It looked as if Willi would break the silence. He looked sidelong at Paule and then at Antek. He was tempted to do his duty as a Hitler Youth member, but he was also tempted to show courage and to talk where the others had been silent. "Mr. Nagold," he began and thought he could hear his heart pounding in his voice.

"Shut up!" Paule hissed from behind him.

Willi stopped talking. Maybe it was better after all not

to let Nagold be the first one to hear about it.

Nagold realized that he wouldn't get anywhere this way. "Come upstairs first. It doesn't make sense for you to be so stubborn," he said, still patiently. "All right, where were you?"

Antek suddenly sensed the teacher's exhaustion and resignation in his patience. "We are sorry that we're late," he said with a firm voice, "but we can't tell you the reasons."

He didn't wait for Nagold to object but went into the music room with calm, sure steps.

"Antek," Nagold's face looked more confused than irritated.

Antek stopped. "Yes?" he said politely.

His friends looked at him with admiration. Now that Antek had set things in motion, it was no longer hard to say no. Antek even had the courage to look Nagold in the eye.

"Is that all?" the teacher asked.

"Yes, sir." Paule gave the answer. His uncertainty had also become defiance.

Nagold's face seemed to grow more narrow. The lines alongside his mouth deepened. He limped a few steps to the boys and suddenly began to bellow, without looking at the children. That was perhaps the strangest part, he was shouting and looking over their heads, somewhere into the distance.

The boys drew back. They hardly understood the words Nagold was yelling at them. Zick was the first to run; he disappeared into the auditorium. Willi and Paule followed as quickly as their pride would allow. Only Antek remained calm and as the last one in quietly closed the door after him.

45

Nagold stood alone at the head of the stairs, breathing hard. Pain wracked the stump of his leg. Had he gone mad? He could still hear the echo of his rage between the walls. He dragged himself along the corridor to his apartment. An old, tired man who thought he saw in his students' resistance a further proof of his own failure. The cup of ridicule was filled to the brim; he had been shot and crippled, put in the power of someone like Jähde, and was despised and mocked by his students.

Confused, the children stood around in the room.

"Why did he yell like that?" the boys asked Antek and his friends.

"He's sick," was Antek's unrevealing answer. "He's probably in pain."

"Where were you?"

"We went to see if the Russians were here yet," Paule snarled.

The student in charge of the class gave out the sheet music. Nothing could be done with the four boys today. They didn't even speak to each other, they brooded to themselves.

Willi was the least affected by the run-in with Nagold. He was still full of his mission to report the Jew, the despoiler of the people and the race. It wasn't that Willi had a worse character than his friends, even though he had no sympathy for the boy in the cellar. Willi had received a perfect National Socialist education. At his birth, his father held a high political post, and when he was eight, his mother put a uniform on him. The first words he learned, to the delight of his parents and relatives, were "Heil Hitler!"

His parents had put him in the boarding school very

reluctantly, because it was known for its unpolitical education. But Jähde had a name in the Party. They trusted his good influence. The boarding-school choir was widely known, and their son had tested above average in singing ability.

Willi was leaning far forward on his bench. His mouth was hanging open. He was drawing little prison bars on the desk.

Paule was calculating, sitting with his legs drawn up on the window seat, and drawing too. But not prison bars; he was drawing numbers. They'd have to offer the Jew a deal. Maybe a couple of sausages. Then perhaps he would disappear quickly and without a trace, as he had come. Jews were supposed to be good at doing business. If only Willi wouldn't act so crazy with this idea of reporting him. Maybe they could make him see reason later. If only Willi didn't have the key, things would be easier.

Paule had forgotten his anger at Antek. He looked over at his friend.

"Antek?"

"What is it?"

"If you hadn't ruined Paule's deal at lunch, then you'd have the key now and Willi couldn't do a thing."

Antek shrugged his shoulders. "All you think about is eating!"

"Of course," said Paule, "that's supposed to be what keeps us alive."

Antek turned his back on Paule. He had no desire to talk about sausages. He could still feel Ruth's reproachful look. She had expected him to defend the stranger against his friends. He had preferred to wait.

Actually, I behaved as Nagold has done his whole life,

he suddenly thought to himself. Observing, waiting, not doing anything one way or the other. Ruth was braver. Was she with the Jew now? If she crawled up to the cellar window, she could look in at him. This idea made him fiercely jealous. Who was this dirty Jew, anyway? He decided to run and find Ruth in his next free moment to talk with her.

5

THE SILENCE OF THE CELLAR was full of noises. Abiram stood motionless and listened. There was a muffled scratching through the chimney in the masonry. It came from the stovepipe on the wall on the second floor. A spigot dripped at regular intervals. Now the intervals were getting shorter and the drops larger. Abiram roused himself. Maybe a pipe had burst in the cellar and within hours everything would be flooded and he would drown. He tried to find the source of the dripping. Behind the shelves the dark was impenetrable.

He saw a large black spot up on the wall. That must be water, that's where the dripping was coming from. Abiram swung himself up onto a wall ledge and from there to a board. He could touch the cellar ceiling and the spot. But it wasn't water. It was just that the plaster had fallen away there. The dripping had to come from somewhere else. Abiram crawled down again. He lay down on the potato crate.

Above him, sausages and slabs of ham hung on the wall. The sight of them made him feel nauseated. The smell of the smoked meats became a stench. The rows of stewed fruit and jam were tightly packed.

Abiram squeezed his eyes to look at them. The stewed fruit jars became people, the little raspberry juice bottles became guards, the shelves became a gymnasium.

That's how they had stood, men, old people, women, children. Day and night, dead people along with the living. He saw the guards swinging their clubs. The dripping in the cellar turned into shots in the gymnasium. The scratching became blows from the sticks. The mice's squeaking became the cries of children. There lay the old man, with a screaming child clinging to him. A woman kicked him in the face. More blows rained down, people were counted, it stank of garbage, blood, and disease. If only the old dead man had shut his eyes. He was staring.

Abiram saw his mother. She was brave, she was young. She had discovered a side door in the corner which wasn't always guarded. She hoped to flee through it and escape death. Abiram covered his face with his hands. He knew what was coming. His mother would try to get through the door with him. But behind it there were guards with whips and revolvers. "I saw you get shot, Mother," Abiram murmured, "don't do it again. There's no escape." But his mother wouldn't learn. She shook her head, she even laughed and waved. She open the door, and at the same moment she cried out: "Abiram! Abiram!" It was as if a shot had hit her cry, her voice became softer. He could no longer see her. "I knew it," he sobbed, "why do you do it over and over?"

The whispering didn't stop. Abiram sat up. There it was, "Abiram, Abiram!" very quiet, somewhere. Horrified, he pressed his hands to his temples. Was his mother following him now even when he was awake?

"Abiram," he heard again.

"No, Mother, no!" He staggered, senseless with horror, to the slat door. He saw Ruth's face pressed against the bars of the cellar window. Her braid had slipped through the grate.

"Abiram," her voice was impatient, "why didn't you answer me? You can see that I've come back." It wasn't his dead mother who had called. The girl had returned.

"Shove the crate against the door, then you can get up on the shelves more easily," she suggested. "There's a slat missing at the top, you can at least put your head through."

Abiram shoved the crate against the door and now it was easy to climb up on the shelves. He knocked a bottle of raspberry juice over with his foot.

"What was that?" she asked nervously.

"The guard," Abiram answered, and stepped on the shards.

"What?" Ruth leaned farther through the bars.

"A bottle of raspberry juice," Abiram said more loudly.

She laughed. "There's enough of that in there."

"Yes."

"Why didn't you answer me?" she asked again.

"I was asleep."

"But you were talking!"

"I do that a lot when I sleep, because I always have the same dream."

"What dream?"

"About my mother being shot."

Ruth grabbed the bars tighter. "You dream that every night?"

"Yes, I'm used to it. But when you called me, I thought I was hearing Mother's voice while I was awake. That scared me."

Ruth couldn't answer. It was terrible, what he was saying. "My mother's dead too," she finally said. "Buried alive."

Abiram nodded as if her information were a matter of course.

"Can you let me out of here?" he asked.

Ruth shook her head. She reached for her braid to pull it through the bars.

"Don't take your hair away," he said. "It looks so pretty."

So she left it, although she could hardly keep her head in that position and the sharp stones of the rubble cut into her knees. He had it much worse down there in the cellar. "I could maybe bring you something," she said, "a blanket, for instance, or a jacket."

"Do you think your friends will turn me in?"

"No," said Ruth, although she was by no means certain. "I don't think so, as long as Antek is around."

"Is that the one with the key?"

"No, the big one."

"But the one with the key," Abiram's eyes seemed to bore through her, "he'll do it?"

Ruth cleared away a couple of stones. "There," she said, "now it's more comfortable for me."

The sun had disappeared behind the clouds. Abiram was hardly visible in the cellar.

"Climb down, behind the sacks of potatoes there are candles and matches."

Abiram didn't want to. "I'll save them for later, when you're gone."

52

"You know," said Ruth, "my grandfather is a good man. He's helped a lot of people. If I tell him about you—"

Abiram pressed his forehead against the slats. "Don't tell anyone anything about me if you want to help me. No grown-up, promise me that."

His eyes looked fearful. He stood on tiptoe to be closer to her. "Please promise me!"

"All right, but . . ."

"You have to promise unless you want them to put me in a camp or shoot me."

"No, I don't want that," she said quickly, "but I have to go now, otherwise someone will notice something, if I'm gone so long. Grandfather will ask me where I've been."

"And you'll tell him nothing?"

"No, if that's how you want it."

She stuck her hand through the bars and waved to him.

"Goodbye!"

"Goodbye!"

She had hardly gotten up when she heard him call. She bent down to the window again.

"I don't know your name."

"I'm Ruth," she said and waved again.

Julius Kimmich's room was shabbily furnished. The windows were so small and the shadow of the granary so dark that Kimmich had to keep a lamp on even during the day. On the kitchen table, where he worked, were piled books, music, and paper. There were two chairs, a table, and a sideboard. Between the windows hung a Biedermeier clock. Long after their old house was destroyed, Ruth had dug it out of the ruins with Antek.

Kimmich looked at this clock again and again. He was waiting impatiently for Ruth. For half an hour he had been looking for a page from the Peace Motet. Antek had been there this morning to pick up folders of music, but Kimmich couldn't imagine that he had taken the music for the motet along too. Kimmich knew what it would mean if that music fell into Jähde's hands. He would have to figure on losing his last source of income as a copyist. That would mean working on the street, clearing away rubble or digging out trenches.

The sound of the garden gate closing interrupted his thoughts. Ruth was home. She busied herself in the kitchen to warm up her grandfather's barley coffee. It was late and she was afraid of his questions. Could she find something Abiram could use in the cellar without her grandfather noticing?

Kimmich joined her in the kitchen.

"Have you seen Antek?"

"Yes, we met at the fountain and watched the wagons for a while," she lied.

"Did Antek mention having taken the wrong music?"

Ruth didn't know. At the moment she didn't care. It seemed more important to her to find a blanket for Abiram.

"Come, help me look," said Kimmich. "I really don't know where to look anymore."

Ruth leafed through the papers. Who knew where Grandfather had put the music? There was such a mess on the table that she gave up looking.

"Did you find it?" Kimmich asked.

Ruth shook her head. "It's probably gotten put in another folder," she consoled him.

She went to the sofa and removed the light rug that was covering it. "It will look better if I fix the hole. It needs a patch."

Kimmich wasn't listening. The missing music made him more and more nervous. Ruth folded up the rug. Grandfather hadn't noticed that. Now she had to find a jacket or a coat.

"Up in the attic we have an old suitcase with clothes," she said. "Couldn't we give some of them away?"

"Yes, if you know anyone," Kimmich answered. "What made you think of that?"

"I saw a boy today with the refugees. He was sick and didn't even have a coat," Ruth said and let her imagination run free.

Suddenly she interrupted her description. "Listen, Grandfather, is it true that when you've lived through something horrible—I mean something you can never forget—that you dream about it all your life? Every night, over and over?"

"Who told you something like that, Ruth?"

"I heard it at the fountain. A woman said it."

"Yes, it's true," Kimmich said. "But you shouldn't hang around the fountain all the time. The suffering you see there doesn't help you. It just makes you sad."

"It must be terrible to have a dream like that all your life," Ruth whispered.

"Go see if you can find something. There won't be much of use up there. And then run over to the boarding school, to Antek. Ask him about the music. If he has it, have him bring it right back to me so there's no trouble."

"But first I'll look for a jacket." Ruth was glad her grandfather was so unsuspicious. If she hurried, she could bring Abiram the things and then go right to the school to ask about the missing music.

There was chaos in the auditorium. When the children had been unable to get anything out of Antek, Willi, Paule, and Zick, they had turned to their music. They had to figure that Nagold would return at any moment and start practice.

"What's this?" asked a voice near Antek, who was shocked out of his thoughts.

"Peace," the boy read aloud, "Quartet for voices, Opus 14, by J. Kimmich, based on a poem by H. Hesse."

Now all the boys were paying attention.

Everybody wanted to see the music.

"Who was at Kimmich's today?"

"I was," said Antek. "Show me that."

It was true. This piece of paper must have gotten mixed up with the other music by mistake. Antek knew the quartet. He had even sung it once with Paule.

"Kimmich isn't supposed to compose music," a young boy crowed.

"He can't perform it, but he can write as much as he wants," Antek replied angrily.

A student grabbed the piece of paper out of his hand and ran to the grand piano. He began to play choppily and with difficulty.

The children groaned. "That's no music! No wonder he's not allowed to have it performed."

Antek ran to the piano.

"Stop that, you can't read music, right?"

He lifted the boy from the piano stool and motioned

56

to Paule. "Come on, sing with me, you know this too."

Paule, who wanted to make up with Antek, came gladly, Zick trailed along. First they rehearsed quietly, then Antek gave the signal to start.

> When peace was everywhere,
>   no one seemed to know
> How sweet its waters,
>   soothing grief and care.
> Now the name of peace sounds
>   weak and low.
> Sounds so far away,
> Sounds so full of tears.
> No one knows when comes its day.
> All desire it soon, and hold it dear.

The boys sat in their desks and listened to the song.

"Sing that passage again," a student interrupted. "That's wonderful, we ought to sing something like that in church!" Enthusiastically he looked over Antek's shoulder at the music. "Who else can sight-read?" he called out. "Until Nagold comes we can sing this. Maybe he'll like it."

"But nothing by Kimmich is supposed to be performed," Willi protested.

Several students agreed with him.

"I think it's a question of the music and not of the political views of the composer. After all, Kimmich was once principal of this school, you seem to be forgetting that!" Antek said it loudly and clearly. He seemed to be trying to make it up to Ruth that he had let her down. "All set," he raised his hands and gave the signal. Still cautiously, but then with their usual sureness, the voices joined in.

When peace was everywhere,
no one seemed to know. . .

Nagold's yelling in the hall had reached as far as Jähde's office. He hadn't been able to fathom the strange behavior of the teacher. Already the fact that Nagold had used his own discretion in allowing a mother to remove her child from the boarding school had made him suspicious. And now he was yelling out in front of the auditorium; there could be no justification for that. Jähde had made it a rule to follow up on every questionable situation immediately. That was the only way to keep things under control, to destroy the evil of danger before it could take root.

The stairwell was empty. Jähde looked at the stucco on the walls. After the final victory, he wanted to replace it with modern murals. Maybe down in the entrance they could hang a picture of him as principal, in his uniform, and thus begin the proud series of school principals of the Third Reich. Jähde loved to imagine things like that. In times of distrust and struggle they refreshed his soul. A while passed before Jähde heard Kimmich's motet. He had been listening to the euphony of the notes for a long time and with the hand that had just closed the window in irritation, he had unconsciously been tapping the rhythm with mechanical precision against the window bars.

When peace was everywhere,
no one seemed to know . . .

Jähde's waking dream burst like a soap bubble. What kind of music was that? That wasn't part of the National Socialist repertoire, and it didn't belong to Nagold's

58

beloved sacred music. Jähde's musical instinct showed him the way. This could only be a composition by Kimmich. Jähde knew Kimmich's music well from the time when he was a teacher under Kimmich. His first burst of admiration had quickly turned to envy, and Kimmich owed it to Jähde's hatred that his choral compositions had been denounced and banned as decadent music.

Jähde yanked the door open. At first the children didn't notice him. In the foreground several of them had crowded around Antek, who was sitting at the piano. Their eyes were on Antek, who knew this music. Now he signaled Paule to chime in; the two were singing alone. Jähde's steps pounded through the music. It was as if he wanted to smash every sound with his feet. Antek didn't have time to hide the music.

"How did you get this music?" asked Jähde.

When he spoke so quietly, it was always a sign of special danger. Zick, who was standing closest to him, closed his eyes. Was there no end to today's bad luck? He could already feel the principal's hand on the top of his head.

"Well, where?"

"I don't know," Zick stammered, "I've never picked up the music."

"It was Antek," Willi interrupted.

He had pushed his way to the front. He clicked his heels together and tried to make his words sound like a report. He ignored the disapproving mutter from his classmates. His cheeks glowed in the expectation of further questions. But Jähde had heard enough.

"So," he said to Antek, "you were the one!"

"I must have taken it along by mistake, sir."

59

Jähde made an impatient gesture. "Still, you can sing it just fine, can't you?"

Jähde continued, "You come to me, you want to play soldier more than anything, but you're really hanging around with miserable defeatists like this Kimmich and then you even sing his little song about peace. Did he put you up to that?"

Antek could hardly contain himself. This bloated pig deserves to be slugged in the snout, he thought. "No, sir," he heard himself answer politely instead, "I haven't seen or sung this music before, no more than any of the other students."

Willi cocked his head to one side as if he had been waiting for this lie from Antek in order to correct him. But he didn't get that far. A stabbing pain shot into his buttock and seized hold.

"We found the music in our folders and we were just sight-reading because we were curious," Paule answered instead.

Willi could no longer bear the pain. He reached around behind him and felt Paule's hand, which was firmly pressing a nail through the seam of his pants.

"So," Jähde drawled, "you were just sight-reading. Somehow I doubt it."

He came to Willi. "Did you sing along too?"

The nail dug in harder.

"No," Willi groaned.

Jähde held the sheet of music in front of his face. "Come on! Let's see if your friends were lying."

Paule pushed the nail a little farther into Willi's buttock.

"When peace was everywhere, no one seemed to know . . . !" screamed Willi.

Paule was merciless with the nail. Willi's voice was smothered in tears.

Jähde tore the sheet out of his hands. "Since when do you bawl like that?"

Willi wasn't capable of speaking a single word. He stumbled over to the piano with both hands pressed against his throbbing buttock.

"But he sang it right," Paule said in triumph.

Willi was breathing hard. His glance promised Paule a thousandfold revenge.

But Paule just showed him the point of the four-inch nail and then pulled it a thumb's width further out.

"Just wait," he whispered.

Willi shut his eyes.

Jähde thought he was just wasting time with the students. It was time to go see Nagold and to find out why he didn't stop the practice and whether he knew about the singing of Kimmich's chorales within the boarding school. He punished the children with a writing assignment that would keep them quiet and left the music room with the feeling that he was finally on the trail of the real relationship between Nagold and former Director Kimmich.

6

THE FARM WAGON with the sick man lying on a pile of straw got just as far as the fountain. Then a tire came loose and clattered against the stone wall. A woman climbed out from inside the wagon, leaned tiredly on the horses' backs, and bent over to look at the wheel. The rim was split. The woman knew that they wouldn't be able to go on with that damage.

"It's all over now," the farmer heard her thin voice saying to the strange girl they had taken along. He turned painfully onto his back. It was good to die when the wagon wasn't rumbling along. If only death didn't fool him again. Every time the wagon stopped he thought he might be allowed to die. He closed his eyes and thought about home.

The farmer's wife lifted up the tarpaulin that covered the wagon frame. Light chased away the warm dark around him.

"Now we're stuck," she said grumpily. She pulled a few pieces of straw from the stubble of his beard.

"I want to die," the farmer whispered angrily.

"Oh, you say that every day and you're still alive. Over there," she pointed at the boarding school, "that big building, that's bound to be a hospital. They'll operate on you there and cure you." She let the tarpaulin fall again.

Now she'll go to the hospital so that I'll be cured, he thought in rage. He raised his head and heard her dragging step. He blinked. Through the gap in the tarpaulin he saw from below the head of the statue on the fountain and thought it was a statue of the Führer. He could see the white traces of pigeons on its shoulders.

"You see," the farmer muttered, "now they've crapped on you too." He lay down in such a way that he didn't see the head with the bird droppings. "But that's no reason to let you look into my coffin." He rolled onto his side again. He was comfortable in that position, but the straw poked him in the face. Why had his wife gone to the hospital when he was already lying in his coffin, in one he had brought from home? I haven't yet touched foreign soil, the farmer thought, I am still at home.

He opened his right eye and saw crates, sacks, bedclothes, and his coffee jug. For almost twenty years he had taken that jug with him every day into the fields, had stilled his thirst from it or in winter had drunk warming whiskey from it. It would be nice to have a last sip before dying. The farmer had neither eaten nor drunk for days.

The strange girl reached under the tarpaulin to find her rucksack. It was time to look around for another wagon. With that split wheel there wasn't much hope of going farther with these people. She didn't want to disturb the farmer on the straw, so she felt around carefully for her belongings.

The farmer saw the white hands reaching through the

tarpaulin. It seemed a little uncanny to him. He hadn't believed that he was going to have to look at Death in the flesh. He lay stiff and stared. If only I had my coffee jug. The hands came closer and closer, up to his feet. Now they were stretching out fingers and grabbing the rucksack.

Irritated, the farmer sat up. He thought he could hear the dragging steps, the voice of the doctor and men with a stretcher. He called out, but it was only a whisper. So he stamped hard on the white hand. Horrified, the girl screamed. She flung the tarpaulin back and looked into the gray face of the farmer. Sweat was dripping from his beard stubble, and his lashless eyes darted about aimlessly. She became afraid and looked around. The wife wasn't back yet.

The farmer moved his lips. "Give me the coffee jug that's hanging on the stanchion."

The girl crawled into the wagon but found nothing because she didn't know what a stanchion was. "I don't see anything," she protested. "Your wife can find it for you, I have to be getting on."

The farmer shook his head vigorously. He scooted sideways to show her that he wouldn't let her out of the wagon until he had his jug, unless she wanted to crawl over him. Finally she saw a dented enamel jug on the top post of the wagon.

"You must be getting better," the girl said and handed the man the dented jug. "Get well," she called and was out of the wagon in one jump.

The woman had stood in front of the boarding school only for a moment. She was convinced that this building with the large windows must be a hospital. Nagold came limping down the stairs. He didn't pay any attention to the women. Every day strangers came into the building and asked for food and shelter.

He had first wanted to go to his apartment, but the idea of finding Margot there, crying in fear among the half-packed suitcases, had held him back. So he wandered through the corridors, pursued by the knowledge that he had lost Antek's love and trust.

"Are you the doctor?"

He looked at the round face of the woman who had just come in. Her oily hair was combed straight back. Her knot of hair stuck up stiffly under the wool scarf. "My husband is sick," the woman said in her Silesian dialect, without waiting for Nagold to answer. "The doctor at home said there was something wrong with his intestines and he won't last much longer without an operation. We wanted to get to my sister in Kassel. Every day he's sure he'll die. But now the wheel has broken on our wagon and the caravan from our village has already gone. So I thought you could help me, sir, so my husband won't die."

"I'm not a doctor," Nagold said when the woman paused for breath. He didn't know whether the woman irritated him or moved him with her simplicity.

"Where is the doctor then?"

"What doctor, for God's sake?"

"The doctor for this hospital!"

"This isn't a hospital, this is a boarding school, a boys' choir school, we teach singing here."

"You teach singing," the farmer's wife repeated and looked around at the high walls. "Then my husband will probably die after all."

"Can I help you?" Nagold asked. Maybe he could at least give the poor woman some advice.

She put her hand on his arm and drew him out the door. "If you help me, if you find me someplace to stay, sir. Just so my husband can have his operation. I will give you my wagon along with Liese, the horse. Maybe you'll want to get away too, when the Russians come?"

She pulled Nagold around the wagon and tried to make the flight attractive to him. After all, he was going to give her his apartment and tell her the name of a doctor who would operate on her husband.

"My dear lady, what do I want with your horse and wagon? What kind of nonsense are you talking? You've got to see to it that you get to the next town and to a hospital. The one here has shut down."

Her glance went back to the boarding-school building as if it held salvation for her husband.

"I'll give you the wagon for nothing, sir, and the horse along with it."

"Ah, that's interesting. Horse and wagon for nothing! Does our music teacher want to run away?"

Jähde was standing behind Nagold, Kimmich's music still in his hand. "Maybe your suitcases are already packed?" Nagold, who at first had wanted to laugh, felt terror rush through his body. Had Jähde found out about Margot's plans to flee? He looked questioningly into the face of his superior.

The farmer's wife had understood nothing. She listened to Nagold's explanations and took it that he definitely didn't want the wagon. So she plucked at Jähde's sleeve.

"Maybe you would like my wagon and my horse Liese," she said, but she soon realized the hopelessness of her offer. In her despair she pulled the tarpaulin up and cried, "Look, sirs, look how sick the man is!"

Jähde and Nagold stared into the wagon. A man lay there on his side, straw in his beard stubble and the remains of whiskey poured over his face. He was dead. The woman bent over him. She picked the straw from his face just as she had done before. "Maybe," she said softly, "maybe one of you gentlemen would take my wagon and my Liese for a coffin and a little plot of ground where I could bury my husband?"

Jähde said a few kind words to the woman and suggested that she should register at the refugee camp. Nagold went back to the boarding school. Jähde followed him immediately. He was suspicious because he had noticed Nagold's fright when he had mentioned the packed suitcases. Why shouldn't this be the time for a little unobtrusive checking-up?

"I'd like to talk to you, Mr. Nagold, can we go to your apartment?" Without waiting for an answer, Jähde climbed the stairs to the apartment.

Mrs. Nagold had not yet succeeded in putting things back in their old order. When the corridor door shut and her husband and Jähde were standing there, it didn't do much good that she was just able to hide a few pieces of clothing under the couch cover. The cans of food which she had nimbly kicked under the cupboard rolled slowly out and landed against Mr. Jähde's feet. He acted as if he hadn't seen her horror and bent over politely.

"Ah, lard," he said softly.

He walked around the room and looked at it. He saw the bulging sofa cover where the clothes were, the suitcase, the sorted papers, and the ashes in the oven.

"You've burned a few things, I see," he said, again in

a charming voice. He weighed the cans in his hands like a juggler before his performance.

"What is it you want?" Nagold asked with forced calm. He could no longer stand by and watch Margot's fear. Mesmerized, she had followed Jähde's movements, her head drawn down between her shoulders as if she expected to be beaten.

Jähde slammed the cans down on the table. "I'll tell you exactly what I want! I want to remind you that for a week now, you're only permitted to leave the city with the personal approval of the district leader. Or have you forgotten about this ordinance?"

"Of course not," said Nagold.

"Well?" Jähde pointed to a packed suitcase, "what's the meaning of all this, if you know about it? Of course you're also aware that the punishment for violating these rules is very severe?"

"My husband has nothing to do with this," breathed Mrs. Nagold. She moved protectively to Nagold's side and looked Jähde bravely in the eye. "I packed because I was afraid. My husband knew nothing about it. When he came in just a while ago he said I should stop. That we didn't need to leave, that we had to remember our duties here."

She clutched her handkerchief and passed it from one hand to the other. "And anyway I'm already unpacking everything," she added.

"How am I supposed to know that?" Jähde asked with a sneer.

Nagold meanwhile had gone around in the room and begun to clean up, as he had done that morning. The books on the shelf, next to them his picture, in uniform, laughing and standing squarely on two healthy legs. He took it down again and looked closely at it.

"Do you really think that this kind of suspicion breeds confidence?" Nagold asked Jähde. He put the picture back next to the books and handed Margot a pile of underwear that was still on the floor.

"Take that into the bedroom."

Mrs. Nagold disappeared, glad to escape the dangerous confrontation.

Nagold had asked his question calmly and coolly, without a trace of hostility. It sounded more like curiosity. Jähde sat down without being asked and began to smoke.

"My dear Nagold," he said. The cigarette bobbed up and down in the corner of his mouth as he talked. "Do you think I enjoy chasing down every detail? Sometimes I would rather just let things go as you do. But if I don't keep an iron hand on the reins now, if every suspicion isn't investigated and even the smallest resistance punished immediately, then we are running a real danger."

Only now did he remove the cigarette from his mouth. "And I, my dear Nagold, am one of the men on whom the Führer can count at home."

Jähde raised his voice as if he expected Nagold to agree. He did, but not quite as Jähde had expected.

"No one doubts that," Nagold said indifferently, "but I don't understand why you choose to investigate me and my wife for subversive acts."

Jähde noticed the sarcasm and regretted his candor.

"Unfortunately, I have reasons," he said in a steely voice.

Nagold, who had stood opposite him the whole time, looked at him inquiringly.

"All right," Jähde moved onto the offensive, "I'd like to know why you were standing on the street chatting with refugees instead of holding choir practice as scheduled, and why your wife is packing."

Nagold felt his will weaken under Jähde's threatening questions.

"Antek, Paule, Willi, and Zick were absent," he obediently replied. "I didn't know where they were, and I can't start practice without their voices."

"Do you know now where they were?"

"No," Nagold hesitantly admitted, and his face darkened because he was thinking about the shameful confrontation with the boys.

"But I know!" Jähde said very loudly.

Mrs. Nagold opened the door cautiously to hear what was happening in the living room.

"You do?" Nagold asked in amazement.

Jähde held the music so close to Nagold's face that he could hardly read it.

"The boys were at Kimmich's! They rehearsed his newest compositions there and brought the music back with them so the others could learn it too. You knew exactly where they were, Nagold. For years you and Kimmich have been thick as thieves."

Nagold had evaded Jähde's gesticulations. "No," he said, "I don't think the children were there." He read the title on the music. "Ask Mr. Kimmich himself."

"I will. I don't need your invitation to do that."

Before Nagold could respond, Jähde stormed out of the room.

7

AFTER HIS RELEASE from prison, Kimmich had never again been allowed to enter the boarding school. Usually the music he copied for the choir was picked up by one of the students. So when a boy arrived this afternoon with the news that he was to report immediately to Mr. Jähde, Kimmich knew that Jähde had gotten hold of his motet music.

"Right away?" he asked, hoping to gain time.

The boy nodded zealously. The principal was already waiting impatiently, he added in confidence. He would have liked to tell everything he knew, but Kimmich didn't give him the chance. He stood at the door impolitely and said, "I'll be right there. You can tell the principal that."

Kimmich was scarcely able to hide his anxiety from the child. But as soon as he was alone, the memory seized him. It had been night, and a policeman was standing in front of him. Like the student today, the policeman had come at the request of Party Comrade Jähde. Kimmich hadn't yet been to bed. On his desk were choral excerpts from "Judas Maccabee" by Handel which he had just worked through in preparation for a large musical evening. Without saying hello, without a word of explanation, the policeman had come in. Kimmich knew him well, since his brother had been one of Kimmich's best students some years ago.

"Won't you tell me what it means that you're here so late?" Kimmich asked, somewhat amused. The thought of personal danger was the farthest thing from his mind.

"Don't get familiar with me," answered the policeman and strode arrogantly around the room in his boots. He pulled open drawers and closets, threw books around, and did everything he could to create an incredible mess in the shortest possible time.

"Haven't we had enough of this farce?" Kimmich spoke with vexation. It hadn't escaped his notice that the policeman's impudent behavior was covering up his uncertainty and that he kept glancing furtively at the door, as if he were expecting someone.

"No, we haven't had enough," answered Jähde instead of the policeman in a cutting voice. "He's doing his duty!"

And Jähde was in the room with those words. It looked as though he had been standing just outside the door the whole time, waiting for his cue. Now he went to the desk, and judging by the complacency on his face, Kimmich deduced that Jähde had found what he was looking for.

"That's enough to get him arrested."

Jähde handed the music to "Judas Maccabee" to the policeman for safekeeping.

"Are you crazy, Jähde?" cried Kimmich.

But Jähde, embarrassed for Kimmich, only averted his face. "Why are you making difficulties, Kimmich? It can only hurt you."

The policeman placed a piece of paper on the desk. "The municipal employee J. Kimmich is hereby placed in preventive custody, since there is a possibility that he may act contrary to the interests of the National Socialist state and its institutions," Kimmich read.

Then everything happened in greatest haste. He was allowed to take along some toilet articles but no clothing or underwear. He wasn't even allowed to take the picture of his dead wife. Handcuffs were clamped around his wrists, and a short time later he found himself in the municipal jail. He sat there for days and nights without being allowed to speak to anyone, without knowing where this arrest would lead. Wordlessly his meals were shoved through the door, and his request that he at least be allowed to speak with a lawyer was greeted with contemptuous laughter. After a week of tormenting uncertainty he was transported away in a police car without being able to inform his daughter or any acquaintances. But that was all only a harmless prelude to what awaited him in the concentration camp. It began with the interrogation. A gigantic SS group leader hit him on the head with a whip. That was to encourage him to make a good, complete report. He didn't understand. A second blow landed on his throat.

"Confess!" bellowed the group leader.

Kimmich muttered his name, address, and profession.

"Louder!" the whip hit again. Kimmich repeated what he had said, but he made the mistake of giving his profession, truthfully, as "principal of the boys' choir academy."

Groans filled the interrogation room. Other SS men had joined the first, they were overcome with laughter.

"Well, then sing something for us, you boy's principal," they roared.

One of them started to pull the clothing from Kimmich's body until he stood completely naked in front of them. The group leader shouted for order.

"You had your little boys sing banned music, you deceiver of the people! And you refused to place your choir in the service of the National Socialist state!"

Again the whip landed.

Kimmich had shut his eyes.

"Answer!" the group leader shouted.

"Yes, sir," said Kimmich.

"All right," the group leader grinned contentedly, "he's learning to open his mouth. But listen now. We want to hear this Jewish caterwauling."

He took a bundle of papers from the desk and thumbed through it. "This whore's song is called 'Judas Maccabee.' Unfortunately, we don't know it. So," he approached Kimmich, "start singing, or I'll give you the pitch!" He raised his whip.

Kimmich no longer knew whether he was singing or not. It was more of a gurgle.

> Oh freedom, sun of life,
> Seat of virtue, source of joy!
> Without you life holds no charms,
> No pleasure worthy of the name. . .

Then he collapsed under the rain of angry blows and the insufferable indignity. He no longer heard the group leader bellow out with his wavering voice as he kept time with the whip on Kimmich's naked body:

> Go forth, you hero! Break apart
> The heavy yoke of slavery!

The clock on the wall chimed five. Kimmich shook his head to clear away the memories. Now he had to go to Jähde, and perhaps he would have to endure torment like that again. But this time Kimmich had a weapon. In the camp he had withstood the acid test of deepest moral degradation. Apart from his own willfulness, he owed his life to his comrade Dressler.

Kimmich, with shaven head, had been assigned to the group of political prisoners, and sewn onto his prison clothes was the red triangle that marked political prisoners. One of the least political men in the world, he had dedicated himself exclusively to music and to building up his choir. He had believed that politics belonged to those who felt called to it.

The coincidence that both of them came from the same town had brought the men closer together. Dressler, as an experienced prisoner of many years' standing, introduced the newcomer Kimmich to the group. Here Kimmich learned that talent is not enough to give a life meaning. Kimmich discovered with astonishment that despite his music, he had been living to no purpose. He was ashamed that it took the most extreme danger to his life to bring him to this discovery. Dressler and his group had voluntarily exposed themselves to this danger in order to build a better world.

For the first time in almost three years, Kimmich entered the boarding school. His former office was recognizable only thanks to the plate with "Principal" on the door.

The bookshelves filled with literature on music had disappeared from the walls and a life-sized picture of

75

Hitler as well as the bust of the youth director for the Reich had taken their place. Next to the window was a map of Russia. The line of the front during the victorious year 1942 was carefully marked with pins and a red string. On the desk, where Kimmich had worked for nearly fifteen years, there stood a miniature version of the Führer's banner.

Nothing in this room called to mind music or even creative activity. A quick glance showed Kimmich his music for the Peace Motet. Jähde tried to cover it with his arms and didn't get up from his chair behind the desk. He was looking forward to surprising Kimmich and to enjoying his fear.

"Before I get to the reason for your visit," Jähde began, "I would like to talk with you about your past. You still remember the reason for your preventive custody?"

"Yes, your denunciation."

"Your impudence, Kimmich, seems to be in much better shape than your memory. I hope that won't cause us difficulties."

He had let Kimmich stand in the doorway.

"You were arrested because you composed decadent music in violation of the law. You practiced Jewish music with the boys' choir even though you received a warning at that time from me as a party member."

Kimmich let Jähde talk without interruption. Silence was the best defense.

"If I remember correctly," Jähde continued, playing with the little banner on his desk, "a year and a half ago you were released by the Christmas amnesty of our regional director and allowed to return home. Were you the only one who was released?"

Now Kimmich sensed danger. What did that have to do with his music? He had to gain time.

"No, there were about thirty of us."

Kimmich's calm answers began to irritate Jähde.

"I don't mean how many were pardoned. I mean who was released to this town with you!"

"Arthur Dressler."

"The Communist pig?"

Kimmich didn't know what Jähde was after. It looked as if he was just using the music as an excuse to question Kimmich about Dressler. Kimmich acted innocent, but the name of his friend alarmed his whole nervous system into wakefulness. The regulation that stated that prisoners were not to maintain any kind of contact with each other after their release had not kept him from staying in close contact with Dressler. Dressler had immediately resumed his Communist political activities. Kimmich had helped him several times by passing on material or news. But after a short while Dressler had disappeared in order to avoid being incarcerated in a concentration camp again. At that time he had broken off all contact with Kimmich. If Dressler had been caught now, that meant that Kimmich would be arrested at the same time, since it was one of the Gestapo's habits to pick up the whole gang in cases like this.

"I asked you whether Dressler is a Communist."

"We all belonged to the group of political prisoners. As far as I know, Dressler was a Biblical scholar."

Kimmich had to smile to himself at these words, because Jähde's question had proved that Dressler was still free. Otherwise Jähde would not have asked with such hatred whether Dressler was a Communist.

Jähde had turned nothing up with his questions.

"Did you know that there's a warrant out for Dressler's arrest again?"

"No!" Kimmich acted surprised.

As if by accident his glance fell on the map and lingered on the Soviet Union. "He always said things were better over there." Without paying any attention to Jähde, Kimmich went up to the map and stuck the pins in such a way that the front line ran through the middle of the Greater German Empire.

"Yes," Kimmich continued slowly, "he was probably not the only one to think that way." He wrapped the string carefully around the last pin. "I assume that you have nothing against this little correction I've made."

"You just watch it! This time you won't get away from me!" Jähde sputtered.

Kimmich had succeeded in luring Jähde out of his ambush. Now, in rage, he would give away the real reason for this interrogation. He watched with satisfaction as Jähde grabbed the music from the desk.

"You dared," he shouted, "to teach the students of the boarding school your pacifist tralala!"

"I am not forbidden to compose, Mr. Director," Kimmich answered politely, "it's just that my music is not allowed to be performed, and this prohibition has been honored to this very minute. The music was brought to the school by accident. The children will confirm that for you."

Jähde had himself under control again. He held the sheets of music between his fingers and while he watched Kimmich with a sneer, the only sound was the crackle of the paper as he tore it.

"You see," said Jähde as he ripped the music into tiny

78

scraps, "that's how simple it is for me to get rid of you. This time you'll land over there where things are better faster than you think."

Kimmich bent his head and Jähde, who took this gesture to indicate fearful submission, could not see the smile on Kimmich's weary face.

"Get out of here," he said, "and count the hours you have left!"

When Jähde had closed the door behind Kimmich and had turned toward his desk again, the red string marking the new front line glowed at him.

8

BEYOND THE TOWN WALL, in what had been the new section, a soldier lay among the ruins. He was tired, but hunger and the increasing cold kept him from sleeping. He looked over toward the town.

This is like lying in a cemetery here, he thought, and tried once more to find a comfortable position on the angular stones. If only I weren't so hungry, but with my uniform I don't dare ask for bread in town. Deserters are shot or tied to lampposts on the market square as traitors and criminals. And on the front the German soldiers are being shot down. And anyone taken prisoner is supposed to starve or be beaten to death or sent to forced labor camps in Siberia. Day after day we have been fed these words instead of bread. Probably to squeeze the last drop of fighting spirit out of the men. If we no longer have any desire to fight for Führer and fatherland, then at least let us fight out of fear.

The soldier in the ruins had no desire to fight either for Führer and fatherland or out of fear of being taken prisoner. He was a deserter and he wanted to go home to his wife. He had run away days ago. It hadn't been very difficult. But every German was an enemy when you were on the run. A refugee woman had hidden him in a haystack on a farm. Children had found him, and people had chased him with pitchforks. He could still hear the farmer's daughter yelling: "I'm ashamed to be a German!" From this time on the soldier had avoided people.

If only I had another jacket, he thought, then no one would guess I'm a soldier. I could go to the public soup kitchens as a refugee, drink hot coffee, eat bread, and sleep on straw.

Twice the soldier had tried, under cover of darkness, to come by civilian clothes. But both times people had shown up before he could rob his victim. The last time it was an older man with a coat made of good material. The man's face had turned yellow when the club had come down on the back of his head.

With a sigh he let himself fall backwards onto the stone. When it got dark he wanted to travel on toward home. Suddenly he heard noises. He flopped over onto his stomach, his club in one hand, an empty pistol in the other. His last bullet had been fired at a Russian.

Ruth was running along the path through the ruins. She had promised her grandfather to ask Antek about the music. Since he had let her look for the old clothes, she didn't want to disappoint him. The shadows of the mountains of rubble lay black in front of her. It was hard to survey the landscape in the dusk. She thought about Abiram, who dreamed every night that his mother was being shot to death. Ruth looked over to the edge of the town wall, where she had lived with her mother before the bombings. Her father had been killed at the very beginning of the war. She could hardly remember the night the bombs fell. She had been about to go to the cellar with her mother when it started to crackle and crash around them. The wall suddenly looked like a piece of wrinkled cloth, and her mother plunged down the stairs in front of her. She didn't remember anything else. Neighbors said that she had been buried alive for many hours. Her mother had never been found. But she had never dreamed about it. Ruth ran faster.

At first the soldier had only heard the footsteps. Now Ruth's form was clearly visible against the evening sky.

"A woman," he muttered, "that's all I need."

He crept as far forward as he could. Now he was lying on the stone wall and could see the narrow path clearly. This is a good chance, he thought and straightened up. But what did he want with women's clothes or a woman's coat? It was pointless.

Suddenly he squinted. What the woman was carrying had to be blankets or pieces of clothing.

Silently he slid to the ground. His hands felt mechanically for a stone. He only had to wait until she was close enough. He started to sweat, his breath came fast. Spittle collected in his mouth. What if he should miss, what if he should only wound her, what if she should scream, what if people were following her? His hand dropped the stone. Slowly at first, then with increasing speed, it rolled down the wall. It bounced and rolled until it was carrying a whole avalanche of stones along with it, which buried the path.

Ruth stood still in terror. She tried to calm herself by thinking that it was only a rock-slide. She clutched the jacket and blanket tighter and busied herself with climbing over the stones that had buried the path.

The soldier knelt silently. At any moment her head

would appear right beside him, and what she was holding in her arms was a blanket and a man's jacket. He could see it quite clearly. Fate must be on his side. He would have liked to laugh aloud. It was like in the movies. Night after night he had been sneaking toward home, hungry and freezing. He had been in hiding because he couldn't get hold of civilian clothes, and here in the midst of dead men and stones a woman comes along bringing him what he's been wishing for. He leaned forward and raised his hand to strike. The blond braid down Ruth's back shone.

"Oh, Abiram, is that you?" Ruth called softly.

Only then did she see that it was a strange man.

"Hands up!" he barked at her and held his empty pistol to her chest.

"Why?" She didn't raise her hands but instead grasped the jacket and blanket more firmly. Her voice was trembling but she crept closer to him until she could see the beads of sweat on his forehead. His hand tightened momentarily around the club he had wanted to strike her down with, but then he let it drop.

"Aren't you afraid of me?" he asked rudely.

"Of course, but Grandfather always says that doesn't do any good."

"He's smart, your grandfather."

"I know."

Only now did Ruth see the uniform, and she couldn't imagine how the man had gotten here.

"Are you a soldier?"

"I was a soldier."

"What are you doing here in the ruins, where nobody lives?"

"You're here too, and I'm not asking you why."

83

He measured the jacket with his eyes. It looked like an exact fit, it might be a little tight, but that didn't matter.

"Give me the jacket!"

Now Ruth understood. He wanted the jacket because he had run away from the soldiers. Instinctively she sensed danger, let herself slide down the wall, and ran off as fast as she could over the stony path. The soldier was quicker. He caught up with her, grabbed her by the braid, and pulled her to the ground. Her forehead stung where it scraped against stones.

"My friends are coming behind me! And if I scream, someone will find you!" she cried in desperation. She was covering the jacket with her body. The blanket had been dropped on the stones. It was getting darker and darker. Fear began to choke Ruth. The soldier's face was very close to hers.

He had to figure that one of these friends would show up at any moment. "If you don't give me the jacket, it's all over for me. Either I'll starve to death, or they'll hang me as a deserter. Do you understand that? But I want to go home to my wife."

As he spoke he pulled on the jacket until Ruth had to yield to him.

The soldier, happy to have a man's jacket, laughed. He grabbed her braid again and turned her head to face him. "What, so young and you've already got a fellow?"

"It's not a fellow. It's a Jewish boy my age who has to hide just like you unless he wants to be hanged!"

The soldier let go of her braid.

"A Jew," he murmured uncomprehendingly, "you're hiding a Jew, you little kid. Are you that brave? Do you know what they can do to you for that?"

"Yes."

The soldier couldn't grasp it. "A Jew," he said again -and shook his head.

"Couldn't you give me your jacket?" Ruth asked hesitantly.

"My jacket? An Army jacket?"

The soldier couldn't believe he was hearing her correctly.

"Yes, that doesn't matter. The main thing is it will keep him warm," she said.

"That's got to be the craziest thing I've ever heard, a Jew in a German Army uniform." He laughed and slapped his thigh. "A Jew dressed up as a soldier, well, more power to him."

He unbuttoned his jacket, took it off and exchanged it for Kimmich's old jacket.

"All right, I'm going now," Ruth said.

The soldier and his laughter made her uneasy.

"Wait, girl, not so fast. First you can arrange something for me to eat or I'll turn you and your funny Jewboy in."

"You can't do that. You're a deserter yourself."

"Oh well," said the soldier bitterly, "you're absolutely right."

Suddenly Ruth felt sorry for him. "Can you jimmy the lock to a cellar? I could get you plenty to eat then."

"Is it a padlock?"

"No, a real lock, like on a door."

"Yes, I can. Why?"

"The Jewish boy is locked in a cellar and can't get out."

"I'm not a fool!" the soldier said. "I'm not going to get caught for the sake of a Jew!"

85

"But he's locked in a pantry that's stacked to the ceiling with sausage and smoked meat."

`The soldier whistled. That was something else again.

"Okay, listen," he said, considering, "first the sausage, at least one of them, and then I'll help the bastard escape from the bacon."

Ruth knew that there was no other possibility of help for Abiram. Since she had to get the music from Antek before dinner, she set out for the cellar as fast as she could.

Abiram had found the candles and had stuck them in a circle on the potato crate. He had shaken the wood out of a sack and wrapped the sack around his shoulders. But it hardly warmed him. With a little piece of wire he scratched the Jewish star into the wood of the crate. He drew each line out until the sign was complete.

Was I born just to be beaten to death? he thought, or why do we Jews exist?

The call of a little owl interrupted his thoughts. Abiram listened. The questioning "kiwit, kiwit" came closer and closer.

"Did I scare you again?" Ruth asked through the silence.

He recognized her face between the iron bars.

"A little, but not much."

"The screech-owl is our signal. You should remember it." She reached her hand through the bars. "Come up here, I have something for you!"

He took the candles and fastened them to the upper end of the slats, to the right and left of the hole.

"Now you look like a saint," Ruth laughed.

"Yes, all that's missing is the Jewish star that your

friends took away from me. But look, I drew a new one down there on the crate so that I don't forget it or anything."

Ruth pushed something soft and gray through the bars.

"You'll be surprised!" She twisted the thing together vigorously. "Now see if you can get it."

Abiram stretched still further. The tips of his toes were smarting and it was hardly possible to force his arm and head through the hole.

"Now you've got it!" Ruth called. "Pull, but slowly, so it doesn't tear."

A warmly lined jacket from the German Army unfolded before Abiram's eyes.

"Is this for me?" he stammered.

"Of course."

"But I can't wear this jacket!"

"Why not, it'll keep you warm."

His fingers brushed over the national emblem with the swastika.

"But I'm a Jew," he said, and all the melancholy of the outsider lay in his reply.

"Yes, you're a Jew," Ruth repeated angrily. "You don't get any more or less cold than anyone else. Take it. Who's going to see it anyway?"

She told him about her encounter with the soldier. How he had threatened her and tried to take grandfather's jacket away from her until in desperation she had suggested the trade. "I told him," she continued, "that I knew of a pantry and that he could stuff himself if he broke the lock."

"And?" Abiram's eyes gleamed. He forgot that he didn't want to wear the Army jacket. He dropped the wood sack from around his shoulders and slipped the warm jacket on.

"He's willing to do it, but I'm supposed to bring him a sausage first, he said. So that he can see I'm telling the truth."

"Did you tell him anything about me?"

"No," Ruth lied.

"That's funny, about the sausage," Abiram mused, "if he had wanted it, he would have come along with you."

"I don't think so. He's just being very cautious because he's afraid."

Abiram climbed down from his crate and got a sausage from a hook. It wasn't easy to hand it up to Ruth through the cellar window. He tied it to a broomstick he found in a corner. Carefully he poked the stick toward Ruth. She was lying flat on her stomach and had stretched her arm as far as it would reach through the bars.

"Just a little higher," she gasped.

But the sausage slid down the broomstick as if it were on a cable railway and hit Abiram in the face.

"You've got to put a nail in the broomstick, then it'll work better."

But they had neither nail nor hammer.

"He's got to have the sausage or he won't help us," Ruth said impatiently.

Abiram remained calm. He tied a cord to the broomstick and tied the sausage on the cord. That ought to work, he thought. He could climb up again and reach the broomstick across to Ruth. But as he slowly let the sausage slide down, the cord came undone. The sausage lay out of reach between the partition wall and the window.

"Does anyone know how many sausages are hanging here?" Abiram asked and looked down into the darkness.

"Yes, Paule, he always counts everything," Ruth whispered. She could hardly speak. "If the soldier doesn't let you out now and a sausage is missing . . ."

"Oh, don't worry," he tried to console her, "I've been beaten so often that once more doesn't matter."

"Get another sausage," said Ruth.

She didn't want him to see her fear.

"And what if it falls into the dirt?"

"Then we'll try it again." She smiled. "The boys won't know that I was involved, and you'll be long gone by then."

Before Abiram succeeded in balancing a dangling sausage and passing it to Ruth, two more had fallen into the small space between the slatted wall of the pantry and the cellar window. The candles burned down to tiny stumps. Abiram wasn't able to cling to the wooden wall any longer. His muscles were cramping from the exertion.

Finally, he fell in an exhausted heap onto the crate, slipped and hit his face on the wood just where he had scratched the Jewish star with a piece of wire earlier. He lay there for a moment. His nose was bleeding. He sat up.

"Hurry!" he called up to the window, but Ruth had already disappeared.

The soldier was getting impatient. If his hunger hadn't forced him to wait, he would have been off long since. Had the little girl turned him in? Maybe it would have been smarter to go with her. On the other hand, the story with the Jew was so strange that the girl couldn't have made it up. It got darker and darker. The soldier crept to the opposite heap of stones. The terrain was less easy to survey over here. In an emergency he could just jump over the crater in order to get away, shielded by the bent iron struts.

Finally he saw her approaching in the dusk. With one jump he moved from the wall down to the path. "What took you so long?" he barked at her rudely. Then he saw the sausage. A lovely, round, juicy salami. His mouth watered. So the girl hadn't been lying. There was a Jew in this somewhere. But that was secondary. The sausage was the center of all his thoughts.

"It's the biggest one," Ruth said proudly.

The soldier swallowed. He took it from her, smelled it, and closed his eyes. His teeth tore at the skin, and gradually his cheeks filled with the salty-spicy meat.

"Now we've got to hurry, it's just going to get darker," Ruth interrupted his smacking bites.

A civilian jacket and a salami, the soldier thought without listening to the girl, that's got to be plenty for two days. Nothing more could happen to him. Why should he run the risk of helping a Jew?

"What are you waiting for? Come on, let's go!"

"Why me?" the soldier grinned. He bit into the salami again.

"You promised!"

"Oh, I promised, did I?" The soldier made a dismissive gesture. The grease on his chin gleamed. "What haven't we been promised!"

Ruth held him back with both hands. "I brought you the sausage! You can't just leave now!"

"Why can't I?" he laughed and shook her off. "Greet

your Jewboy for me. The sausage was just the right thing for a starving soldier!"

He jumped onto the wall, then across the crater behind the iron struts.

Ruth could no longer see him.

9

ANTEK HAD MANAGED to leave the boarding school after practice. He picked a route through side streets, because he could have been seen if he had crossed the market square to the granary. Here, with all the crannies and alleys, no one noticed the boy. In the first twilight there was a great deal of activity in the sheds and cellars. Handcarts were being packed, crates nailed shut, sacks hidden. Now and then a door opened and another refugee joined the great trek west. Although the punishment for leaving the city became more and more severe, that didn't stop people.

Antek noticed little of all this. He was trying to find Ruth. He wanted her to explain her strange behavior. He wanted her to tell him why all it took to threaten their friendship was some Jew wandering in. He crept along in the shadows behind the granary until he reached Kimmich's house. "Kiwit, kiwit," he called out, but nothing stirred. Antek jumped over the fence. He knocked on the window and the door and finally called Ruth's name. No one came.

He stood in front of the house, completely at a loss. He began to feel hurt that Ruth was not at home. The thought that she might be with the Jew, keeping his spirits up or even helping him, nagged at Antek.

Over and over he tried to figure out the reason for the innocence with which she had taken the stranger's part today. She had acted as if the Jewish law didn't exist! Antek crouched on the steps. He let the gravel run through his fingers. Maybe it wasn't innocence on her part, but a challenge instead? Maybe she had just wanted to show off. To show how brave she was compared to him, who had been afraid of showing sympathy in front of Paule and Willi. The pebbles of gravel landed like shots on the steps. He threw one after another, as if by doing so he could get rid of something that was stirring in him, deep and displeasing.

Antek shook himself. "Why aren't I allowed to be a soldier?" something shouted in him. Why couldn't he fight for Ruth, for the refugees, for his fatherland? He wanted to fight so that there would be no "nothing," as Nagold had said. Every day the radio droned out that the Führer needed every man and boy to bring about the final victory. But he had to be locked up in a boarding school, singing day in and day out, and now he even had the aggravation of that Jew who'd wandered in like a stray dog. Antek felt as if he was smothering. He had only one burning desire: to run away and join the soldiers, to fight, and—if need be—to die.

He imagined himself lying on the battlefield, a medal on his chest, a dead smile on his pale face. Comrades are bending over him and wiping the blood from his forehead. One of them opens his jacket and takes Ruth's wrinkled photograph. A whole handful of gravel rained down on the steps. Antek erased the photograph in his jacket from his fantasy. It would be better to die anonymously. As an unknown soldier.

"Antek, is that you?"

Suddenly Kimmich was standing there; Antek hadn't heard him approach. Antek had a hard time bringing his thoughts in order. "Are you here about my music?" Kimmich put a hand on Antek's shoulder. "One of us must have put it in with the folders by mistake." Kimmich took Antek into the house, sat down, and offered the boy a chair.

"Thanks," Antek stammered, embarrassed. He had been thinking neither about Kimmich nor about the music. He sat stiff as a board on his chair.

"Oh," Kimmich said casually, "don't take it so hard. This whole ghastly spell will be broken soon."

Antek flared up. "Are you starting with that now too?"

Antek looked at the old man, full of defiance and rebellion.

"Starting with what?" Kimmich asked, surprised.

"Talking about the war being lost and everything being over. How nothing makes any sense because there won't be any fatherland to live for anymore."

"Who said that to you?"

"Nagold," Antek continued, "and he also said that it would be ridiculous for me to be a soldier. He said it was better to sing for the dead than to fight for them." His voice sounded higher, and there was a sob in his throat. "But I'm not resigned to that. I want to be a soldier, I want to fight for final victory. Just like the others!"

Antek didn't notice the tears running down his cheeks. "And I didn't even come to see you, I wanted to see Ruth."

94

"I see," Kimmich said, "you were looking for Ruth." He was silent for a moment that seemed endless to Antek. "I've made a mistake."

Antek wiped his coatsleeve across his face. He felt sucked dry. He couldn't even utter a word of apology.

"You can wait here," Antek heard Kimmich saying as though nothing had happened.

So he waited. The clock ticked in the silence of the room; it was the only sound between them.

"You've thrown so much at me," Kimmich finally began, still with his back turned to Antek, "that I just don't know where to begin. If I thought your visit was on my account, you must excuse me."

"I didn't mean it like that, Mr. Kimmich."

"But it's true that you didn't come to see me. Anyway, that's not so important."

Kimmich turned around. "If Hitler loses his war, you don't know what will happen. That's the reason you want to fight. Before everything is lost, you, Antek, want to prove that you can die for your fatherland if necessary."

Antek tried to interrupt.

"I'm not blaming you for that," Kimmich continued. "The desire to defend and to fight for one's country is as old and as proper as humanity itself. But it depends on what you're fighting for. For our people the important thing now is not to die but to live. If you believe that you have a duty to do, then it is to stop any fighting for Hitler, or even to keep others from fighting."

Antek had leaned far forward, as if he were seeing the old man for the first time.

Kimmich sensed the chance he was taking with his words. Antek was a student of Jähde's and he was a

95

member of the Hitler Youth. If he didn't succeed in making Antek see the truth, it could mean death for Kimmich.

"Mr. Jähde," Kimmich continued, not releasing Antek with his gaze, "has good reason to be afraid of a defeat. But you have no more to fear than I do!"

Slowly Antek relaxed.

Kimmich didn't let loose. "A better life has to start for all of us."

The corners of Antek's mouth turned down in what looked like a sneer. "Better life," he echoed scornfully, in a soft voice.

"Yes, better!" Kimmich said sharply. "Tell me what it is you want to fight for now? Do you want to defend Adolf Hitler, at whose command millions of people have starved to death, been gassed, been exiled, been tormented to death? Do you want to die so that the racial madness and the madness of destruction in Germany can continue?"

Antek didn't understand Kimmich's words. Millions of people have starved to death and been gassed, he kept hearing in his head. "Let's assume," he said, without giving Kimmich a glance, "let's just assume that you're telling the truth, then we have no choice but to fight to the last man in order not to be destroyed ourselves."

"I am telling the truth," Kimmich said, "I can't give you the exact numbers, but this might serve as an example. While I was in prison, eight thousand Jews were gassed just because they were Jews. There was nothing else against them."

"Jews?"

"Yes."

"If that's true," Antek continued laboriously, "then Nagold would be right, then there would be nothing left to believe in."

"Oh, yes there is, Antek, a new beginning, a different beginning. Not with death and destruction but with the will to a new society, in a new order. That's worth fighting for. Do you understand that?"

"No," Antek roared and shoved his chair back. "No, I don't understand it, because they couldn't have been telling us lies for twelve years!"

He ran past Kimmich out through the door.

The washroom provided the students with a place where they could be undisturbed. Except in the mornings and evenings, hardly anyone entered the high-ceilinged, tiled room with the opaque windows. When the wind came from the west, the stale odor of cheap soap was joined by the putrid emanations of the sewers.

While Antek, Paule, and Zick sat on the rim of the bathtub, Willi perched on the window sill.

"I'm sick of telling you a hundred times! Of course you have to turn a Jew in."

In his thoughts Antek could hear Kimmich's voice— about eight thousand Jews were gassed during my imprisonment alone. "That's your opinion, Willi," he said calmly. "But it's our business too, so you have to listen to our opinions."

Willi slid down from his seat at the window. "As if there could be any other opinion. Either I'm a Jew, then I'm out of luck. Or I'm not!" He lifted his head. "And then I'll fight against this inferior race before I get damaged by it myself."

Willi sat down with his friends. Since neither Paule nor Antek confirmed his interpretation of the Jewish law, he kicked his legs angrily until his heel drummed against the tub.

"Be quiet," growled Paule.

"And what's your opinion?" Antek asked him.

"You can think what you want of me, but I still think it's crazy to turn the Jew in. First of all that would mean not having anything more to eat, and second, we would run the risk of being punished for stealing." Agitated, he paced up and down in front of the tub. "You can't ask Paule," he said, "to run a risk like that."

Willi snorted contemptuously. But Paule paid little attention to Willi's disregard. He tapped him lightly on the shoulder. "My sense of duty as a Hitler Youth member doesn't go any further than that."

"All right," Antek said, interrupting the quarrel that was the beginning. "I take it that you don't want to report the Jew. Fine, but then what do you want to do with him?"

"That's just it!" Paule confessed his perplexity. "If we turn the boy in, he'll report us out of revenge. If we don't turn him in, we commit a criminal offense." He nodded toward Willi. "And aside from that he's eating up everything we have."

Antek shoved his hands into his pockets.

"What do you think?" Paule asked, carefully following his plan. He poked Willi in the side in a friendly way. "We could give the Jew a couple of sausages, say, and tell him to get lost."

Paule watched Willi's face anxiously, but his suggestion had only increased Willi's defiance.

"Are you crazy?" Willi kept himself from shouting

with difficulty. "Don't you have even a spark of honor in your whole body?"

"I didn't want to keep my honor alive for the Russians to get," Paule drawled.

Willi had jumped up. He was wounded by Paule's cowardly attitude toward the situation. He would have preferred to stalk away from him, because it was only through people with warped attitudes like Paule's that the enemy had been able to reach German soil.

"Zick," Antek interrupted, "you're pretty little, but you were still there. Your opinion matters too."

Zick, who had not counted on being asked, had been doing gymnastics on the towel bar next to the tub. Proudly, he approached. He looked at Antek, then at the wary Paule and the enraged Willi. He would have felt better if he knew where Antek stood. For the first time he felt the weight of responsibility.

"Well, let's hear it," Paule said impatiently.

"It's not a bad idea to chase him away," Zick said hesitantly, but when he met Willi's threatening gaze, he continued anxiously, "but if we report him or take him to the police, that's certainly the right thing to do."

"It would be best for you to do that yourself," Antek suggested.

Zick looked at him, appalled. "Me? I couldn't do that!"

"Why not, if you think that's the right thing to do?"

Zick squirmed under Antek's question. His pride that they had wanted to hear his opinion melted away. "Because he hasn't done anything except eat that little bit of liverwurst."

"Speak up, Zick," Antek encouraged him. "I think the same way you do."

Willi couldn't believe his ears. The tiled walls spun around him. These traitors were his friends. Not a single one of them had the courage to turn in a dirty Jew.

"And you mean to tell me you want to be a soldier," he exploded. He looked at Antek in contemptuous wonder. "You're a coward, a miserable coward. But I have the key, and I—"

He got no further. Antek's fist caught him in the face. He stumbled back and would have fallen if Antek hadn't grabbed him by the collar.

"You listen, Willi, and listen good. For three years we've been good friends. You, Paule, Zick, and me. We don't want that friendship ruined by some Jewish boy who just happened to wander into our cellar." Antek pulled Willi backwards by the collar to the bathtub and pressed him against the rim.

"I've let every one of you tell his opinion, and every opinion is worth as much as every other one, do you understand?" He shook Willi, who could only see out of one eye; the other was swollen shut because of Antek's punch.

"But," Antek continued as his hold on Willi's collar tightened, "none of us is a coward if he doesn't go right to the police or the block leader with a boy who's the same age as we are. How do you know that Jew has even committed a crime?"

"It's not a matter of committing a crime," Willi growled, "it's because he's a Jew."

"Is that a reason for him to die?" Antek turned Willi loose.

"Die?" Paule asked, bewildered, and even Willi's swollen face showed astonishment.

"Who's talking about dying?"

"I've heard that," was Antek's answer. His voice sounded strangely husky to his friends, so that they believed him without understanding it. Antek looked at them one by one. "I don't want to bear the guilt for an innocent boy dying. Do you?"

"But there's a law. . . ," Willi interjected.

"Oh, a law, just hold on. I want us all to go to the cellar together tonight, you too. We'll be able to find out from the Jew whether he's guilty or not. Then you can talk about your law."

Antek washed his hands. It felt good to let the cold water run over the hands that had just hit Willi. He reached into his pocket to dry them off. When he pulled out his handkerchief, the Jewish star fell out. It fluttered to the ground and lay on the wooden floor grating. Antek picked it up. "Promise me that you won't tell anyone anything about this and that you'll come along with us."

"All right, I promise." Willi didn't look at Antek.

Within the last twenty-four hours, the front had changed. The Russians had succeeded in making a new breakthrough. The almost completely exhausted German division was routed. Only with the help of the Home Guard could a new base be established farther to the west. The stream of refugees swelled to a flood. There was tumult on the market square. People were shouting for lodgings, bread, and coffee. And those weren't the people who had spent weeks and months traveling hundreds of miles on foot through snow, rain, and cold, nor the people whose goal remained uncertain, or even the people who were carrying nothing with them but their own suddenly meaningless fates. These were new arrivals, who had been fleeing only for days or sometimes only for hours. Some of them had acquaintances in the town and demanded special treatment.

"They'll calm down," a woman said as she pulled up her skirt and soothed her raw feet in the fountain.

"Get your filthy feet out of there, that's drinking water!"

The woman looked up in surprise. The man was wearing good shoes, had a backpack and a leather suitcase. Obediently she raised her dripping feet onto the stone rim. "Have you been traveling long?" she asked, with a smile at the suitcase.

"Long enough for me," the man grumbled, "almost two days. And on foot, too. No one can stand that kind of punishment! What about you?"

With a practiced hand the woman wrapped rags around her feet. Then she slipped into her wooden shoes, picked up a pack and said, "Two months!"

10

JÄHDE HAD AVOIDED looking more closely at his military map since Kimmich had moved the red string marking the front. On the other hand, it didn't occur to him to move the string back to its old position.

Now the stream of refugees, unusual at this evening hour, had generated a restlessness in Jähde that drove him to the map. His finger moved along the line of pins, which loomed up from the paper like tiny guns in ominous proximity to the town. Jähde did some calculations. But he was calculating with divisions, tank units, anti-aircraft guns, all of which no longer existed. His finger slid slowly north until it circled a cross drawn in blue pencil.

"Here," Jähde said, tapping the spot with satisfaction, "this is where they'll deploy the V2." There was no other possibility. Once again Jähde began to do calculations and figured that the rapid advance of the Russians was merely a ploy of Adolf Hitler's, who wanted to attack and annihilate the enemy from this spot with the miracle weapon, the V2. The more he thought about it, the more it seemed to him a plan of genius. These thoughts led him to place the red string farther to the west himself. But the new demarcation would mean not death but victory.

The telephone jangled twice before Jähde awoke from his dream of playing general.

"Heil Hitler," the rasping voice of District Leader Hoffmann greeted him from the telephone and informed him that at present there were five hundred refugees in the town, looking for lodging.

Jähde took the news calmly. Times of utmost stress often created such situations. However, the plan that District Leader Hoffmann was describing did not meet with his approval.

"There are still three hundred people without shelter. I'd like to put them up in the boarding school."

"In my school?"

"Yes. You have room enough in your classrooms. And then you have the auditorium. A hundred people can sleep there easily."

"How are we supposed to conduct our classes?" Jähde protested.

"That isn't important. Sing in the church for all I care, or just forget about it. In any case, the refugees will be quartered in the school. Heil Hitler!"

Jähde had to make the best of it. Two hours later, three hundred refugees from the market square pushed and shoved their way through the wide-open entrance doors of the boarding school and occupied classrooms and corridors for the coming night. The zeal with which they dragged their possessions up the stairs, piled them against the walls, sat down in front of or on top of them, checked the size and shape of every nook and cranny to find the best place, reminded Jähde of a swarm of termites. That very morning he had been imagining where his portrait as principal, in uniform, could be hung. Now the refugees' last belongings were piled up on that spot. The walls were being scratched up, and the building rang with the shouts and calls of these strangers who took possession of every room and every object as if it were their perfect right. They created a tidal wave of restlessness that swallowed up everything in its path.

Suddenly Jähde understood that it was more important now than ever to stand his ground. To give in to the panic all around him would be treason and would undermine the final victory. His orders were exact and considered. Gradually the situation of being in charge of several hundred people, even for a single night, began to give him some pleasure. He instructed Nagold to take some students and clear the dormitory and give the beds to elderly and ailing refugees. The boys had to make do with blankets in the smaller classrooms. The corridors were to be kept free of baggage to allow free movement through them. Refugees were not allowed to enter the kitchen without his permission. Special requests like warm milk, tea, or hot water were to be made to Mrs. Nagold, who would be assigned assistants as she needed them. Thanks to Jähde's efforts, there was soon some order and peace among the refugees.

In contrast to the upper floors, it was quiet in the cellar, where the boarding school kitchen was. Mrs. Nagold had not been present when the three hundred people arrived. She had been downstairs making a large kettle of peppermint tea. The students passed the tea among the refugees. Only the scraping of feet penetrated into the cellar, but it sounded as threatening in her ears as the nightly grinding of the tanks' chains.

With a sigh she threw a few handfuls of dried leaves into the seething water. The sharp odor of peppermint brought tears to her eyes. She didn't know which was making her feel sick, the fear or the smell: Russians, refugees, tanks, packing, peppermint tea. Ideas and images chased through her mind like flashes of lightning. She opened her eyes and saw Zick standing there, looking at her with his head cocked.

"What is it?" She felt as if he had caught her being derelict in her duty.

"Nothing," Zick said, "I only wanted to see if I could help you. Nobody has anything for me to do upstairs. So I just thought I'd come down to you." He lifted his head and sniffed the air. "It smells down here!"

"Yes, it certainly does," Mrs. Nagold said. A smile played across her face. She stirred the tea until it had to be poured.

"Hold the pots for me, would you?"

Zick held buckets and pots while she filled them. Then he carried them to the stairs, where they were taken by other students.

"Do you think my parents will come soon and get me?" he asked as he held another bucket for her to fill.

Mrs. Nagold lowered the ladle, and the tea splattered over the edge onto the floor. "Of course your mother will come. She could arrive any day. You mustn't worry about it."

She pulled Zick to her. How could she have forgotten how eagerly the children awaited news from their parents?

"You don't think they'd leave you here if they have to flee," she tried to console Zick. "My God, what a big hole you have in your sweater. I'll darn it for you. How did that happen? Did you hurt yourself?"

Zick was speechless. The unaccustomed display of tenderness by Mrs. Nagold dumbfounded him. He couldn't recall her ever hugging him or one of the other boys. Whenever he had torn a hole in his clothing before, there had always been a punishment but never the question about whether he had hurt himself. He looked self-consciously from the puddle of peppermint tea to Mrs. Nagold's troubled face. It embarrassed him to be comforted by her.

He had asked about his parents because he was thinking about Abiram and what would happen to him. Zick was certain that his father would be able to give his friends good advice, but he was just afraid that his parents would get there too late.

He began doing his work again, energetically dragging the teapots over to the stairs.

"Do you know," he changed the subject, "that there's a fortune-teller upstairs? I saw her. She reads the cards for you if you give her something. Do you think everything that she says is true?"

"That's forbidden, Zick!"

"All right, but she's doing it anyway," he answered impatiently, "and a lot of people say that what she says will come true."

"Would you like to know where your parents are?" Mrs. Nagold asked softly.

Zick sighed. Now she was going on about his parents again. When all he was interested in was what they should do with the Jew, especially because Antek had said he might be killed if they turned him in.

"You mustn't listen to such talk. No one can predict the future. If you want to know something," she said, and her voice again had that soft, shy sound, "then come and ask me."

"Then please tell me," he asked, "what happens to Jews when you turn them in?"

Mrs. Nagold's face, which had just shown traces of maternal love, contracted and became stiff and guarded.

"Those are things," she blurted out, "that you don't even think about, let alone talk about."

Zick's question had shaken her. "Go upstairs and don't come down here again with stupid questions like that!" She wiped up the spilled tea and cleared the kettle of tea leaves. She was sweating with fear.

"Could you please warm some milk for my grandchild?"

Mrs. Nagold looked into the wrinkled face of an old woman who was holding a baby bottle out to her imploringly. Zick was nowhere in sight.

Antek and Paule, who were responsible for clearing the dormitory, had arranged it so that their and Willi and Zick's new sleeping places were in the same room. After they had been sent to bed, they had propped open the door to the hall. They wanted to be able to tell when it was quiet enough in the halls for them to sneak out unnoticed. For the moment that wasn't possible. In the corridor of the second floor, not far from the stairs, the fortune-teller had yielded to pressure from several people and had begun reading the cards. A couple of suitcases had quickly been turned into a table, and a stable lantern furnished enough light for the woman. She didn't look at all as one would picture a fortune-teller. She was no old woman with wild hair, gnarled

108

fingers, and dark gaze. She was neither fat nor particularly thin, had neither a hump nor a cat on her back. She was a pretty, young woman with lively eyes.

"My husband," a woman asked with a trembling voice, "is he still alive, will I ever see him again?" She dug around in a purse, pulled out a gold pocket watch, and without a word let it slide into the fortune-teller's lap.

"Does the watch belong to your husband?" the fortune-teller asked without looking up.

"Yes."

The fortune-teller placed the watch on the king of diamonds. Then she gathered up the rest of the cards and flung them face down in front of the woman. "Keep drawing cards until I say stop."

The woman drew one card after another. Her hand would hover helplessly over the cards. She would be about to draw one and then would drop it. She closed her eyes and tried to feel her way to happiness until to her relief she heard the fortune-teller say the word "stop." A bright circle of overlapping cards surrounded the king of diamonds with the watch.

The heads of the observers bent over still closer. No one wanted to miss this moment. Even Mrs. Nagold was there. She hadn't been able to forget Zick's news that there was a fortune-teller among the refugees.

"I just want to see if there's anything I can do," she had told her husband, happy to be able to vindicate herself. Suddenly she had seen this young woman with the cards on the suitcase. Mrs. Nagold pushed her way through the silent crowd. She had the same desire they all had to know her fate. And at the same time the hope that she might avoid it.

"Your husband," the fortune-teller now said with a monotonous voice, as she shoved the cards apart with short, small movements, "he's alive." She continued in short, jerky sentences. "There isn't much time, today, tomorrow, within hours. There is danger unless you find him."

"My God, how am I supposed to find him? Tell me," the woman implored with a choking voice as she stared at the cards.

"He must be with an old man, nearby," the fortune-teller murmured.

"He's with my father-in-law!" the woman shouted. "My God, he's at home with his father. He's alive, he's alive!"

Blinded by tears, she stumbled up, asked no more questions, didn't thank the woman, ran to the stairway. The people around whispered in deep astonishment. The fortune-teller looked up as if she were awakening from a good dream. She looked around with a soft smile, reached for the gold watch that was still lying on the king of diamonds, and yawned.

Mrs. Nagold could no longer resist the temptation to have her cards read as well. But the fortune-teller was tired. No pleading or pressure would help. Only the little crucifix with the real pearls, a confirmation gift from Mrs. Nagold's parents, made the fortune-teller less tired.

Mrs. Nagold listened skeptically. The prophecies of the fortune-teller didn't satisfy her. She was sorry she had to parted with the piece of jewelry.

"A small dark man means danger for you and your husband."

"I don't know any small dark men," Mrs. Nagold said,

annoyed. She felt ridiculous for having been duped by this nonsense.

"There is great danger. You can only avert it if you ask for help in time from a man who is involved with you professionally. Don't forget that . . ."

The voice of the fortune-teller sounded urgent. She took the seven of spades and threw it into the middle.

Mrs. Nagold stood up. "Let's forget it."

Irritated, she walked off, nervously looking around to see whether Jähde or some other member of the school had seen her.

After Mrs. Nagold had gone to bed, Paule, who was standing watch at the door, thought the moment had come for them to sneak out.

"Now we can go," he whispered and nudged Zick, who had fallen asleep during the long wait.

The creaking of the door frightened them, but no one noticed it. Anyone who was still awake was listening to the rumble of artillery in the distance, not to the squeaking of a door.

Willi stumbled against a boot that protruded into the hall. Everything seemed so unreal; a few hundred strangers in the boarding school, the Russians in the vicinity, a Jew who was dependent on their will—and they themselves were leaving the building without one of the adults being concerned. Paule snapped his flashlight on. The circle of light whisked across the figures on the floor to either side. Twisted bodies loomed up ghostly out of the dark.

The four were glad when the building door shut behind them. The market square was peaceful, the fountain murmured. Only the wagons served as reminders of the fleeing people and the press of the day.

"First let's get Ruth," Antek said and grabbed Willi's elbow as he wanted to run off toward the town gate.

"Naturally, the girl has to go with us," Willi mocked. The friends paid him no attention. There was nothing for him to do but go along.

Antek had to repeat his "kiwit" three times before they heard Ruth's voice behind the window shutters. "I thought you weren't coming," she whispered.

"Hurry up," Willi interrupted her.

"But I can't come right away. My grandfather has just gone to bed. I have to wait until he's asleep. Otherwise he'll notice. Can you wait a few minutes?"

"Absolutely not," said Willi. "I have the key and I'm going to the cellar when I want to!"

"Don't be so mean!" Ruth didn't know how she could get away sooner. Her grandfather would be sure to hear the door or the rattling of the shutters.

Antek, who was angry at Willi's showing off, said, "We'll wait for you. Come as fast as you can. We won't go into the cellar without you. I'll see to that!"

Antek was friendlier than he had meant to be. He had by no means forgiven her questionable behavior of that afternoon, but that was no reason for her to have to put up with Willi's boorishness while he was around. He didn't admit to himself that her pleading voice had moved him.

"You're nice, Antek, thank you. I'll hurry."

The boys set out to see Abiram.

Ruth had sensed it. When she finally entered the little corridor, her grandfather turned on his light. The band of light shot out under the door.

"What is it?" he asked.

Ruth didn't answer. She didn't move until Kimmich had turned the light out again. She heard him turn over in bed. If she wanted to follow the boys to Abiram at all, she was going to have to stand there and wait until her grandfather was fast asleep. She sighed and crouched in a corner. She believed that Antek would keep his word and not go down to Abiram without her. Otherwise it could be bad for the Jewish boy. Willi wouldn't believe the story with the soldier and the sausages. Ruth listened tensely. She could tell exactly when her grandfather was sleeping soundly because he started to snore in a regular way.

Ruth pulled her short skirt over her knees. She felt a strong urge to cough. She swallowed. "Dear God, let me not cough," she prayed and pressed her face into her jacket. Finally she thought she could hear her grandfather's peaceful breathing.

Smiling, Ruth pulled the door of the building shut behind her, almost flew over the gravel path of the garden to the street, and nearly tripped. Something lay right at her feet, against the garden fence. A lifeless body! Its legs were drawn up, its head bent down, its back curved toward the street. Its bent arms were clasping a pack.

Ruth's first thought was that she should wake her grandfather. Then she remembered Abiram and the danger he was in. If Willi should find the sausages in the passageway in front of the pantry wall, no excuses would be good enough. Should she endanger Abiram's life because of a dead person? There were plenty of dead people!

Ruth shoved her foot in front of her until she touched the body. Nothing stirred. Let somebody else find the corpse. She had to get to the cellar.

Then suddenly she heard a cry, a little thin, pitiful cry. Ruth stopped without turning around. The cry behind her slowly became the yowl of an infant. Ruth hurried back and knelt down. She parted a tangled mass of hair and saw a haggard, suffering face. Ruth turned the body onto its back. As she carefully took the crying child out of her arms, the woman opened her eyes.

"I've got to go on, I've got to go on."

"Where are you going? Who are you? How did you get here?"

The woman merely moved her lips.

Ruth saw that she had to help her or the woman would die of weakness and the baby in her arms would starve. Running along the narrow path back to the house to wake her grandfather, her thoughts were no longer with Abiram.

11

AFTER THE YOUNG WOMAN came to and the baby was taken care of as well as possible, she implored Kimmich to ask around in town for the caravan from her home town. In the crush at the bridgehead a few miles east she had lost her friends and relatives. The Russians had come closer and closer. There had been shooting, and the agitation at suddenly being alone brought on the birth prematurely. With her last remaining strength she had dragged herself through the streets, and it seemed like a miracle that Ruth had found her.

Ruth didn't look up. "I heard the baby crying," she said by way of explanation, "so I got up and went to see."

Her grandfather suspected nothing. "You saved the baby's life."

Ruth thought about how her foot had touched the lifeless body and how she had wanted to leave it to chance who should find it and deal with it. Were her friends with Abiram now? What would happen to the Jew? The thought that perhaps two people's fate had been decided by her hands oppressed her. If only I could get to the cellar now, she thought, or if I could at least tell Grandfather about Abiram. She was convinced that he would have sympathy and help for her. But then she remembered her promise not to say anything to any grown-up. That was what Abiram had demanded.

"I'm going to the official assembly point now," Kimmich interrupted Ruth's thoughts. "I'll ask about your people. If they're no longer here, at least someone will know where the caravan has headed. You'll spend the night with us."

He pulled on his coat. "My granddaughter will look after you." He nodded at Ruth without waiting for an answer from her.

Now there was no more possibility of getting to Abiram and her friends in the cellar. Ruth made some soup for the woman and heated milk for the baby. She tore some old linen goods into swaddling for the baby and wrapped it up as well as she could. The young woman on the sofa didn't say a word. She followed Ruth's efforts to care for the baby with her eyes.

"Are you cold?" Ruth asked, simply to break the silence.

"No."

The baby was sleeping. Ruth laid it next to its mother. There was nothing more to do but wait for whatever news Grandfather would bring from the assembly point.

Actually Ruth had expected some word of thanks. She was injured by the way the woman took her help for granted. Wasn't it a sacrifice for her to leave Abiram in the lurch and to irritate her friends by letting them wait? Willi, who had never liked her, would now have one more reason to agitate against her. The

116

woman lay there as if she didn't care a bit whether Ruth had saved the life of her child or not.

"At first I wasn't terribly afraid," Ruth suddenly heard her saying.

"My mother always said that when you're having a child you're not so easily frightened. Nature has arranged things well. But at the bridge, where we were all standing crammed together like sheep and had to wait while they started shooting, then I was afraid after all. I think it was a grenade that exploded in our midst. I fell down and lay there because I thought that would be the best way to avoid being hurt. I was stepped on and kicked, but I stayed down. People were screaming and racing across the bridge. I was lying on the ground and I thought it was stupid that the people wanted to cross the bridge while they were shooting. I noticed much later that there had only been one shot and that I was the only one who had stayed down. My people must have assumed that I was dead. When I raised my head all I saw was strangers. A few yards ahead of me I saw two little children holding tight to each other's hand and calling for their mother. They were pushed over the bridge railing into the water by the charging mass of people."

The woman sat up, looked over Ruth's head, and her voice sounded unpleasantly tinny. "No one, no mother, no soldier, no woman paid attention to them. They ran on, they didn't even look down!"

The woman closed her eyes. "Then I got up. I crept as well as I could to the wooden railing of the bridge. All I could see was something bright being carried away. It must have been the skirt of one of the children. Then I started to scream. I didn't want to, but screams came out of me, over and over, and so loud that I held my own ears. I don't know how long it lasted, but suddenly I wasn't screaming with horror anymore, I was screaming with pain. Then I knew that I was about to give birth, and I came to my senses. Someone pulled me aside because I was lying in the way.

"There were fewer and fewer people on the bridge. I can't imagine where they all went so quickly. Part of them came back again and hid in the nearby woods. It was clear to me that I had to find a safe sheltered place if I wanted my baby born alive.

"I forgot about the drowned children, my people, the shooting, I didn't even think about the Russians."

The woman paused. It was as if she herself had to stop and think about how she could have forgotten the drowning children.

"Can you understand that?" she asked softly.

"Maybe," said Ruth.

"I'm thirsty. Is there any milk left?"

Ruth handed her a cup with the rest of the milk.

"Not far from the bridge I found a shepherd's wagon," the young woman continued. "That's where I gave birth, all alone. The baby didn't see the light of the world, it saw only the darkness of a shepherd's cart."

"But how did you get here?" The stories of the young woman were tormenting to Ruth.

"After an hour or two I got up. I wrapped the baby in my shirt and went across the bridge, past Russians, tanks, German soldiers. Two Russians stopped me at one point. They talked at me. I didn't understand a word. I just showed them the baby. They looked at each other and one of them pointed me in this direction. He talked on and on. He pointed in the other direction too, but he shook his head as he did. I just went on. I was much too tired to be afraid of anything."

"Didn't the Russians take you prisoner?" asked Ruth.

"No. I was going toward the town, just as one of them had directed me. Fifteen minutes later the shooting began. I thought at first that now everything was over and I would die with my baby after all. But the Lord held his hand over us, because hardly a shot landed where I was running. Until I got to town."

The woman lay back. "Have I even thanked you yet?" she murmured. "You probably saved my life and the baby's."

"I think," Ruth said hesitantly, "that it was the Russian who saved your life!"

"What do you mean?"

"Well, the one who pointed out the way that would be safest for you to go."

"Are you saying that a Russian wanted to help me?"

"You just told me that," Ruth smiled.

"You think. . ." the young woman didn't finish her sentence. The idea that a Russian could sympathize with a mother and a newborn child was more than she could grasp.

"Up to this moment," she whispered, "I thought it was just a lucky coincidence."

Before Ruth could answer she heard Kimmich's steps. She looked at the clock, but it was too late for Abiram. There was no excuse that would let her leave the house now.

"The caravan from your village is here. I was able to find your people, too, and tell them about you. I'll take you there tomorrow morning. There's no point in going there tonight," Kimmich said kindly.

The woman turned to the wall, took her child in both arms and cried. Without a word, Kimmich pulled the bedclothes up over her.

"Did the baby drink some milk?" he asked Ruth softly.

She could only nod. Contented, he turned the light out and took Ruth with him out of the room.

12

ANTEK HAD SUGGESTED every possible thing that might have held Ruth up. But after they had waited more than a quarter of an hour, freezing in the ruins of Schiller Street, even his patience was exhausted. The friends were very cold in their gym suits. The moonlight raised ghostly shapes and shadows of wild devastation out of the darkness.

"You're probably afraid," Antek said to provoke them, a last attempt to get them to wait a little longer.

"Yes," Zick said defiantly, "I don't want to stand here freezing anymore and wait until the rats eat my feet off."

"The time we're losing could be valuable, Antek," Paule reminded him. He didn't mention that the darkness was making him nervous, too.

"I'm not going to wait here in the middle of the night among all this rubble and these stones for Ruth or for some Jew," Willi said. "I'm going to the cellar now. If anyone doesn't like it, he can . . ."

He marched with a firm step along the path until he came to the ruins of 10 Schiller Street. Paule and Zick followed him. Antek finally gave up, and embarrassed in front of his friends by Ruth's unreliability, he joined them angrily.

When Abiram heard Willi's steps through the cellar window, his first thought was: the Army jacket. He tore it off and stuffed it in the potato crate. He didn't know whether Ruth was along or not, what the boys had decided, whether they were for or against him, or how much they knew about Ruth's attempts to help him. He sat down on the lid of the crate, which he had pushed so that he could keep an eye on the door, and blew out the candles.

The boys quickly rolled away the cement block, which had kept Ruth from going to Abiram that afternoon. Antek cleared away the last obstacles that they had shoved in front of the iron door. Finally the small corridor that led to the pantry lay before them. Paule followed close behind Willi. His flashlight played restlessly over the walls.

"Shine it on the ground, or we'll fall down," Willi complained.

Obediently, Paule shone the light down, and Willi felt his way forward as quickly as he could. Suddenly Paule stopped and held Willi back. They had come to the end of the corridor. To the left they could already pick out the slats of the pantry wall.

"Look there!" Paule whispered. All four saw the salami at the same time, gleaming in the yellowish light. The sausages were lying a few yards in front of them in the corridor as if someone had dropped them while escaping.

"Damn it, now he's gone," Willi shouted. With one jump he was at the slatted door. He pulled the key from his pocket. "You idiots, you numbskulls! It's your fault the Jew has slipped through my fingers. Because of all that business with the girl and Antek's crazy idea of playing at being just! That's what you get! And he looted our pantry too, the pig!"

Willi shook the slatted door, but it was locked. In his anger he didn't stop to think how the Jew could have gotten out with the door locked. He fumbled around wildly with the lock until the door flew open.

Paule, who understood right away that Abiram had to be in the pantry still, had run his light quickly over the whole room. He hadn't missed the figure on the crate. In hopes of giving Willi a shock, he kept quiet. Neither Antek nor Zick had seen Abiram yet.

"There, what did I tell you! He's gone," Willi snorted. He looked for Paule. "Bring your flashlight here!" Paule didn't come. He stayed at the door in order to survey the situation better.

"Why are you yelling in that stupid way," said Antek in irritation, because he suspected Ruth. "We locked him up, after all. Of course he was going to try to escape. I would have too."

"What? You're comparing yourself to a Jew?"

"Stop talking that nonsense, Willi!"

Willi didn't stop. "If I get my hands on that guy, I'll—" He couldn't immediately think of any punishment harsh enough for Abiram. He turned around hurriedly. His extended arm hit against something soft and warm. He screamed in fright. Zick dashed to the door. Paul giggled to himself and held the light so everyone could see Abiram.

"I don't know what you think is so funny!" Willi growled at Paule.

"Oh, you can't take a joke," Paule answered and lit the candles that he found next to Abiram on the crate.

"Just look at Willi, he can't get a single word out!"

"Neither can Abiram," Antek said, "it's really funny."

Zick came back slowly from the corridor. He had the salami sausages in his hands and put them down near Abiram on the crate. "Why did you throw these out?" he asked.

Abiram didn't answer. He tried to peer into every corner to see whether Ruth might not appear after all. Willi had given himself away with his threats, and Abiram felt the growing danger of Ruth's absence.

"It's not up to you to ask questions, Zick," Antek barked at the little boy.

He shoved over an empty shelf that was low enough to serve as a bench. Willi sat down on the outermost edge.

Paule had seen the Jew before he did. His friend had played a joke on him in front of this inferior human being, in order to humiliate him, Willi.

Antek pulled candles out of his pocket. He must have collected them in the boarding school. "Stand up," he said to Abiram. The candles gave a bright light.

Abiram made no move to stand up. He knew the risk he would run if he stood up from the crate that held the Army jacket. Instinctively he sensed that Antek was the only one of the boys who didn't hate him. Nevertheless, he hesitated.

"Stand up," Antek repeated neutrally, "and move over there!"

He pointed to the slatted wall near the door.

Willi wordlessly closed the door and sat back down.

"If you want us to treat you decently, then be good

enough to do as I say!"

Abiram felt Antek's impatience. Slowly he got up and leaned against the wall. He was standing opposite the bench on which the four boys now sat: Willi, with his legs spread and his elbows propped on his knees, his gaze riveted on the victim against the wall, Paule, sitting sideways, a little too nonchalant, Zick expressing tension and curiosity at the same time. He sat with his upper body bent forward, his knees pressed together, close to Antek. Antek didn't know how to go about beginning the interrogation. Abiram stood silent with his head to the side. In his thinness he looked wretched compared to the four well-fed boys. His black hair, hanging long over his ears, shone in the candlelight.

"You can go ahead and look at us, and you don't have to stand there as if we wanted to hang you!" Antek burst out.

Abiram didn't move.

"All right, let's get started," Antek suggested.

"High time," grumbled Willi. "This farce you're putting on here is really stupid."

Antek looked at Abiram. "Before we come to a decision we would like to know some things about you. It's up to you to answer the questions truthfully. I advise you in your own interest not to lie and to give an account of yourself to each of us. That's the only way we can handle this whole matter before us responsibly."

Abiram still didn't move. None of the four boys knew if he understood how much justice they were granting him, a Jewish boy. His silence irritated them.

"What's your name?" Antek began.

"Abiram Rother." He looked at the four boys one after the other.

"Where are you from, what do your parents do, and where are they?"

"I was born in Berlin. When I was six my father was taken to a concentration camp. He was a jeweler."

"What's a concentration camp?" Willi interrupted.

"You don't know what that is?" Abiram asked. He couldn't believe that a member of the Hitler Youth didn't know what a concentration camp was.

"I'm asking the questions here, not you!" Willi barked.

"Then I'll tell you!" Abiram took one step forward so that his worn-out and overlarge shoes were right up against Willi's black boots. He leaned down to Willi until the two were face to face. Willi couldn't escape the smell of Abiram's filthy clothes, he even felt the Jew's breath on his face.

"Get back against the wall!" Willi yelled in disgust.

"A concentration camp," Abiram continued without paying attention to Willi's command, "is a camp where you can get in but you can seldom get out. But you can die in any number of ways."

Abiram came closer still. Willi held him at arm's length with both fists.

"You can be beaten to death or starve, you can be tortured to death or shot to death or gassed, you can get a fatal injection, you can be burned to death, strangled—"

"Stop it!" Willi shook Abiram like a dog and finally pushed him against the wall.

"That's a shameless lie!" Willi screamed, beside himself.

But Antek had already sprung up and pushed Willi back down onto the bench.

"Where is your father now?" Antek asked.

Abiram leaned against the wall and clasped the slats.

"He was gassed," he whispered. His eyes didn't avoid the gaze of the other four.

"And your mother?" Antek forced himself on to the next question.

"She was shot in a gymnasium. I was standing next to her."

Antek turned away. He had no more questions. Abiram's sober manner proved to Antek the truth of what he had said. Ashamed, he realized how ridiculous his undertaking had been, to try to play judge here, and retreated a bit in silence.

Since Antek had no more questions, Paule thought it was his turn. "How do you know that your father was gassed?" he began hesitantly.

"From a *Kassiber*."

"What kind of nonsense is that?" Willi interrupted, because he couldn't imagine what a *Kassiber* was.

"That's a letter or a note that is smuggled out of the camp and passed from hand to hand."

"And why did they do that to your father?" asked Paule, who didn't want to be interrupted by Willi again.

"Because he was a Jew!"

Paule shook his head, dissatisfied. "That's no kind of reason!"

"Oh yes it is, it has been for twelve years!"

Paule looked questioningly behind him to Antek. "Then you were right about what you said in the washroom."

Antek nodded.

Paule felt uneasy and suddenly had not the faintest desire to interrogate the Jew anymore. He turned his palms up as if to say: Do what you want, I don't care.

It was Zick's turn to ask the Jew questions. But nothing occurred to him. He chewed his lower lip and looked sideways at Willi who sat straddled next to him.

"If you can't think of anything, Zick, it's Willi's turn," said Antek.

"Of course I can think of something!" Zick stared at the Jew, perplexed, as if he could read a question from his lips. It wouldn't be much longer before he had proved once again that he couldn't be taken seriously. Anger about Abiram boiled up in him. Why did he have to come into this very cellar? Zick suddenly knew what he would ask the Jew. The significance of the moment lent strength to his voice. "If you were with your mother in the gymnasium and she was shot there, why are you here?"

"Right," Willi burst into the question, pushed Zick aside and planted himself in front of Abiram. "If you were arrested, how come you're free now?"

"Because I want to live, just like you!"

"That's a stupid answer," Willi sneered.

"You think so?"

"Don't get smart!" Willi shouted. Now it was his turn and he would prove to his friends that there were more important things than sympathy.

Zick was the only one still sitting down. He felt superfluous, and while Willi talked at the Jew, he shoved himself off the bench. Abiram's answers echoed in his head. After his mother had been shot dead, that was really not a stupid answer. Zick imagined how it must be to have your mother lying dead beside you and to be all alone. Suddenly it seemed to him that Willi was being cruel.

128

Willi, who took the silence of his friends to be agreement, began again: "You were arrested with your mother and you broke out."

Willi underlined each word by pounding on the shelf with his fist. Jars and bottles rattled. He stepped up to Abiram. "That proves," he continued and placed his leg on the wooden cover, "that through your escape from prison—"

Willi got no further. The lid of the crate, which Abiram hadn't been able to close tightly, didn't hold Willi's weight and snapped. Willi's foot slid off and stepped on the Army jacket. "Well, what have we here?" he cried, pulled the jacket out of the crate and held it up into the light of the candles.

"There you have your proof!" he gloated in a breaking voice. "This Jew is a spy who wanted to soften you up with his fairy tales about his father being gassed and his mother being shot. Or maybe it belongs to one of you?"

"That isn't true, don't believe him!" shouted Abiram. He grabbed Willi by the shoulder.

"Don't touch me, you swine!"

"You're crazy, I'm not a spy. The jacket doesn't belong to me!"

"So," Willi laughed, "can you maybe tell me and my friends how this jacket got here and who it belongs to?"

Abiram's gaze hung pleadingly on Antek. "I can't tell you, but believe me anyway. I am not a spy," and he added quietly, "the girl—"

"Aha, the girl," Willi sneered again, "you miss her now, don't you? Maybe you could fool her. She belongs to the gang of traitors too, but you're out of luck with my friends and me!"

When Antek heard Abiram say "the girl," he knew immediately that Ruth must have been here. He didn't know what had gone on, but he knew one thing: the Jew was innocent.

Antek grabbed the jacket out of Willi's hand. "That's enough of your shouting! We've listened to it long enough. The jacket doesn't prove anything. It was locked in there the whole time!"

Antek went to stand in front of Abiram.

"You've been getting on Paule's nerves ever since you opened your mouth and started spouting nonsense like Jähde," Paule said in a bored tone to Willi and went to stand behind Abiram.

"Now I get it," Willi whispered and retreated step by step.

"You don't get anything," Antek cried impatiently.

Willi was already at the door. Before the friends realized what was happening, he had pulled it open, slammed the door behind him, and turned the key.

"Traitors," he gasped from outside the pantry, "you dirty, miserable traitors, all of you!" It was hard to tell whether contempt or disappointment was behind his words. "You're getting what you deserve."

"Willi," Antek shook the slatted door, "open up and don't do anything silly!"

Willi shook his head. "No," he said, "you can't fool me any longer. You lied. All of you wanted to pull something over on me. But you and the Jew are all in this together. In the washroom you hit me because of him," he sobbed, "and I believed you and thought we were friends!"

"Stop it, you idiot," Paule interrupted in a rage, "and save your sentimental slop. Open up so we can straighten this out!"

"It'll get straightened out sooner than you think." Willi pressed his face against the slats. "I'll have all of you arrested," he whispered, "and you, Paule, I'll pay you back double for that nail. Don't think I've forgotten that."

"You're going to turn us in too?" Zick cried and pressed his hands to his mouth.

Willi tossed the key in his hand. Then he disappeared.

"He's running off!" Zick stepped up to the slats. "He locked us in. He can't mean it!"

Zick ran in circles in the cellar until Antek laid his arm comfortingly around the younger boy's shoulder. "Yes he can mean it, Zick," Antek looked over Zick's head to Abiram, "just like we locked the Jew in." Antek turned to Paule, who had watched Zick's despair.

"Do you see any other difference between Abiram and us?" he asked.

"Yes, I do!" Paule danced around the three, giggling. He drew every drop of enjoyment out of the moment. "There is no difference between you, Abiram, and Zick," he tapped each on the shoulder with a theatrical gesture, "but there is a difference between all of you and Paule!"

"He's gone crazy," Antek sighed.

"Maybe if we all throw ourselves against the door at once, we can break it down," Abiram suggested.

Paule's eyes gleamed with pleasure. "Don't you want to know the difference?"

"Come on, stop it," Antek said.

Paule held a brand-new key under his nose.

"Would you like to smell it too?" he asked Abiram, laughed, and clapped him happily on the shoulder.

131

"Now you tell me, isn't that some difference?"

Abiram stared at him, speechless.

Paule put the key into the lock, opened the door wide, and bowed low like the perfect servant. "If you please, perhaps the gentlemen would enjoy a little freedom?"

"Paule," Antek laughed, "how in the world did you do that?"

He didn't know whether he should embrace his friend. At any rate he shoved him hard in the side. Zick put his arm around Paule and hopped around with him. Paule grabbed for Antek and Antek for Abiram. They all slapped each other's shoulders and boxed around until they were exhausted.

"Where did you get the key?" asked Zick, still out of breath.

"Later," Antek said, "now we've got to get out of here. Willi could come back at any moment."

Paule was disappointed. He had wanted to demonstrate how clever he had been. But Antek was right.

"Everybody take as much of the stuff here as he can carry. So we have supplies for Abiram."

"Where's he going to go?" Zick wanted to know.

"I don't know, but out of here!" Antek's glance happened to light on the Army jacket. He picked it up and dusted it off.

Everyone fell silent.

"Yes, the jacket . . ." Abiram said uncertainly. He couldn't betray the girl.

"Did Ruth bring it to you?" Antek asked haltingly. "It's decent of you not to want to betray her. But under some circumstances this could cost you your freedom or even more."

"Yes," said Abiram.

"You can tell us. You can see that we want to help you."

Paule grunted. Abiram couldn't tell whether that was agreement or rejection of Antek's statement. He trusted no one and continued to be silent.

"All right," said Antek, "if that isn't enough for you, we—I mean Ruth and I—" He paused for a moment and began to lie, "we agreed that she would help you get out of here. We had to pretend otherwise because of Willi. Do you understand now?"

"You and Ruth agreed on that?" Zick asked, astonished.

"Shut your mouth," Antek said rudely. "She did it in the dumbest way she could. I'd like to know what she was thinking of! And she wanted to come with us just now." He looked at Abiram. "She probably has a good reason for staying home."

"What do you mean by that?" Abiram asked.

"It doesn't matter," Antek answered quickly, "we're here now! Why do you think Paule arranged to get a spare key?"

Paule puffed his cheeks full in amazement.

"For the single reason of getting you out of here!" Antek continued.

"That's really something," Paule stammered and held the candle stump up close to Antek and Abiram's faces. He wanted to see what was really going on here and how Antek came to be telling such a pack of lies.

Paule saw that Abiram was smiling trustfully as Antek put a warning finger to his lips. Then he was quiet.

Abiram no longer doubted the boys' honesty. He

described in short sentences what had happened.

"And in return for the sausage," he finished his report, "the soldier was supposed to break open the lock. But neither the soldier nor Ruth came back."

13

WILLI WAS GLAD he had taken Paule's flashlight along. He felt very much alone as he ran through the night, accompanied only by his shadow. The paths among ruins and rubble seemed endless to him. He began to whistle a lively march. But in the middle of the night even this battle hymn didn't raise his courage.

It's crazy to whistle, Willi thought, everyone can hear it. He began to hum just loud enough so that he could hear himself. Willi thought about the day when he was given his Hitler Youth uniform by his father and first put it on. He was eight years old and wasn't yet at the boarding school. It was a Sunday in spring. His mother had a light dress on for the first time that year, and everyone was in a good mood. Willi was really not supposed to put the uniform on until the afternoon, for the swearing-in ceremony that would make him a tenderfoot. But Willi begged for so long that he was allowed to put his uniform on in the morning. The brown shirt, a little too big because it was bought to allow room to grow, and the black pants with belt and shoulder straps. He had rubbed the shiny silver swastika on the belt buckle again and again. Although it was new, it didn't seem shiny enough to Willi. He went into the kitchen and cleaned it until he could see himself in it. But he wasn't allowed to put on the necktie yet. He had to be a tenderfoot for a while before he could wear it. Still, he could try it on. When his father came to breakfast, Willi greeted him at attention: "Heil Hitler!" His father returned the greeting with a laugh, then took Willi's necktie off. "That's not something to play with," he said and put it back in the dresser.

Willi's parents lived near the freight yard. Right behind the house was a heavily traveled stretch of tracks; the embankment was one of Willi's favorite spots. He could sit there for hours and count the freight trains passing by or wave to the soldiers who were being transported from east to west or from west to east. He admired the big guns, the tanks and jeeps that rushed by him. Later he was pleased by the slogan on the locomotives: "Wheels must roll for victory!"

Once a day an express train came by. Willi liked this train the best. If he lay down on the ground a minute before the train was due and pressed his ear against the tracks, he could feel a slight vibration that quickly became a rumble and then a rolling roar. Then it was time for Willi to let himself roll down the embankment so as not to get caught. A dangerous, forbidden, wonderful game. Each time he felt the same thrill at staying close to the tracks until the last possible moment.

So Willi couldn't let even a Sunday go by without going to the embankment, especially because he was wearing his new Hitler Youth shirt with the belt. It was early in the morning, and there was still half an hour before the train was due. But it was a good opportunity to sneak unnoticed onto the forbidden embankment. He sat waiting in the grass on the hill, his hands clasped proudly around his belt.

Finally he heard a muffled pounding in the distance. Willi sat up. That wasn't the express train. He looked in disappointment at the puffs of smoke from the engine of a freight train. But the closer the train came, the more it slowed down, and it stopped in Willi's vicinity with a squeal of brakes. Willi saw right away that it was a livestock transport. He crept up the embankment. Maybe he could find a chink somewhere to peek through. When he got to the tracks he saw SS men with weapons jumping down from the train. They were guarding the doors of the freight train as if something dangerous might emerge from it at any moment. Without giving it much thought, Willi hid himself and remained unseen by the men. He kept completely still. Now he could clearly hear noises coming from the cars. Suddenly Willi understood that this rumbling and groaning in the cars couldn't come from cattle, sheep, pigs, or even horses. It sounded different, strangely alien.

The SS men walked to the other side of the train. With one bound Willi was at the tracks. The signal light showed that the train couldn't pull into the station yet. He had enough time to investigate the matter. As he was standing close to one of the cars he clearly heard a wailing. Suddenly he had the feeling he was being watched. Puzzled, he looked up at the air slot of the livestock car and saw with horror two eyes looking back at him. Willi wanted to flee.

"Don't run away, boy," he heard a muffled voice from the car. Immediately the wailing stopped.

There are people behind those doors, flashed through Willi's mind. On the other side of the train the SS men were running up and down.

"Open the door a couple of inches," someone whispered through the air slot. "We can't get any air!"

Willi stared upwards.

"Hurry!"

It was deathly quiet in the car. Willi went up to the door. He shook it cautiously but it didn't give.

"You have to shove the bolt up!" someone said from inside.

Willi looked around. There was a stick not far from him. He used it to reach the bolt. He pushed with all his strength against it. Now he could see eyes at the other air slots as well. He became frightened. Then the bolt gave and sprang back. A horrible odor assaulted Willi.

Suddenly someone's hand grabbed the back of his neck and turned him around. "What are you doing here, fellow?" bellowed an SS man and dragged him down away from the tracks by the collar. Then things happened very fast. His father appeared within minutes. Without a word he unbuckled his belt and began to beat Willi with it in front of the gateman. Then his father dragged him home. When his mother saw them coming, she started to cry.

"Who told you to fool around with that boxcar?" his father shouted behind the closed door.

"There were people in there," Willi sobbed, "they said they were smothering. They wanted me to open the door a couple of inches."

"Take your uniform off. You're not worthy to wear it. You showed sympathy for that rabble, those traitors to the German people, who were being transported to a labor camp." Willi undressed until he stood facing his father in his underpants.

"Our young people have to be as hard as Krupp steel. The Führer has no use for sissies like you. Remember that!"

His father had sent him to bed while his friends were sworn in to the Hitler Youth.

At this moment he felt just as alone and deserted as he had felt then. The gates of the town were just in front of him. He noticed that he was still humming to himself. Shocked, he stopped, because without being aware of it he had been singing Kimmich's motet:

> When peace was everywhere,
>   no one seemed to know
> How sweet its waters,
>   soothing grief and care.
> Now the name of peace
>   sounds weak and low . . .

"As hard as Krupp steel," something shouted in Willi and he was ashamed that Kimmich's melody had passed over his lips. "As hard as Krupp steel," Willi had vowed to himself when he later became a member of the Hitler Youth. Now was the time to prove how hard he had become. Now his father would be proud of him. Today he wouldn't have to unbuckle his belt and beat him for showing sympathy with traitors to the people. The lesson his father gave him had to be passed along to his friends so that they learned through their own humiliation to become hard.

When Willi's fist pounded against the downstairs door, Block Leader Feller tumbled sleepily out of bed.

"The bell's broken again." He pulled his pants on in

fury and flung open the window. "Go ahead and beat the door down! You just can't wait for me to get downstairs!"

He was astonished when he found one single boy at the door, from the noise he had expected half a regiment.

"Block Leader Feller, I would like to make a report!"

"You rascal, you damned kid, where did you come from? Aren't you from the boarding school?"

"Yes, but that doesn't have anything to do with what I want to report."

"Wouldn't you rather report to Director Jähde?" asked Feller, enraged over the boy's nerve in waking him at that hour.

"Does that mean, Mr. Feller," Willi responded, "that in these grave times you refuse to take the report of a Hitler Youth member at night?"

"All right, all right," Feller said in a conciliating way, "it must be pretty important." He let Willi in.

"Well?" he asked.

The block leader's get-up didn't seem very dignified. His pants were half unbuttoned, and his nightshirt was hanging out. His unshaven face was swollen with sleep, and his hair stood up in bristles. The block leader had folded his short-nailed hands over his stomach. The room smelled of cold potatoes and tobacco.

"Maybe you'll get started sooner or later!"

"I've cornered an escaped Jew!"

"You've done what?" Feller held his head at an angle, his hand cupped behind his ear as if to hear Willi's news better. He looked stupid in his amazement. He cleared his throat.

"It's a sixteen-year-old boy who has a German Army

140

uniform and therefore is under suspicion of being a spy."

The block leader laughed. He didn't take Willi seriously. The whole thing sounded like a practical joke. A Jew in uniform, and then discovered by a boarding-school boy—that struck Block Leader Feller very funny.

"Come on, boy, you don't believe that yourself!" he said. He didn't know what he should do with Willi.

"I locked up the Jew with his uniform in a cellar. Here's the key."

"Where's the cellar?"

"In a ruin on Schiller Street."

Willi could hardly disguise his anger at the laughing Feller. "If you don't want to come with me and you refuse to take charge of this, then I'll go to District Leader Hoffman!"

"Shut up! Who said I wasn't coming along?" growled Feller. With annoyance he shoved open the door to the bedroom and called: "Mama, bring me my uniform!" Then he held his head under the faucet and ran cold water over his greasy neck.

"If you're lying, my boy," he snorted the drops of water from his nostrils, "then you'll find out what Block Leader Feller is all about. Nobody plays tricks on me!"

Willi merely smiled.

A plump woman with a short bedjacket over her flannel gown brought Feller's uniform.

"What is it now? We're not even allowed to rest at night!"

She looked Willi over skeptically.

"You don't understand, Mama," Feller said. He pulled on the brown breeches that his wife held out to him patiently. "It could be a case of espionage," he added.

Suddenly Willi remembered that he had said nothing about his friends. How would he explain their presence when Feller discovered them in the cellar? "A case of espionage," Feller had said decisively. If his friends were arrested along with the Jew, it could be very bad for them. Willi paced up and down, trying to think.

The lesson he had taught his friends by locking them up with the Jew should really be enough to bring them to their senses. Now he had to find some way out for them.

"Let's go," said the block leader.

Willi walked along the path to the ruin in silence. He hardly spoke to the block leader.

"You can see for yourself. Interrogate the Jew. My duty is only to report the matter to you."

"How did you get into this cellar?"

"I was following the Jew. He hid in there."

They passed through the town gate. Willi still didn't know how to keep his friends out of the matter. Suddenly he was very tired. He longed for his bed and wished the whole affair with the Jew were only a dream.

"What was that?" The block leader stood still and undid the safety on his revolver. "Imagination," he said, and walked on.

"Have you arrested many people?" Willi asked, trying to start a conversation.

"You're too curious, my friend!"

"I didn't mean it that way," Willi hurried to explain. "I just wondered what you think about at a time like that."

Block Leader Feller shook his head in surprise. "Why

should there be anything to think about?"

"Yes, of course," Willi was angry at his own question. But what if his friends were arrested by Block Leader Feller along with the Jew?

The silhouette of the ruin was clearly recognizable against the blue-black night sky.

"There!" Willi said hoarsely. He wondered if Zick would cry.

"You go first," said Feller.

Willi crept along the corridor. Maybe he could convince the block leader that his friends were there to guard the Jew.

"Is this fellow alone?" asked Feller.

Willi didn't answer. His heart was pounding. There were the slats, the door, and still there was no noise. They must be very frightened. But only the Jew would come to harm. The Jew . . .

Feller took the light from Willi and shone the light through the cellar. The slatted door stood half open. The block leader pushed it fully open.

Nothing. Emptiness.

"Where do we go from here?" the block leader asked impatiently and shone the light on the walls. It lingered for seconds on a slab of ham.

"Here," Willi stammered, "we're here, this is the place," and he pointed to the door, "this is where I locked them up." He looked around for candles. "Maybe they're hiding!" Willi took the light from Feller and shone it into every corner.

"They have to be here, I locked them in," he whispered, bewildered. But he found nothing, not the Jew and not his friends, and even half the provisions were missing. Feller didn't say a word. Hands on hips, he watched Willi's ridiculous search.

"Maybe your Jew's in a marmalade jar," he said threateningly. "What did I tell you at home?" He boxed Willi's ears. I told you that you'd be sorry if you were lying to me!" And he rained blows on Willi's head again.

"I can prove it!" Willi screamed.

"I can see that. Shut up before I lock you up." And suddenly suspicious, he asked, "Why did you get me down into this cellar anyway? What's this supposed to mean? What's going on here?"

Willi shielded his head with his arms. The block leader wasn't hitting him only because he was angry. He was also afraid of the trap he thought Willi had lured him into. He wanted to beat the truth out of Willi.

Willi fell over the crate and lay there. He didn't care what happened, let the block leader beat him to death. He couldn't do anything more than tell the truth.

"There were three boys from the boarding school with the Jew, they must have helped him escape," Willi groaned.

"So, suddenly we have three more boys. Why didn't you mention them earlier? Are they more Jews in Army uniforms?" Feller pulled Willi up from the crate. "Who's behind this? Why did you lure me down here?"

"I didn't lure you here. Nobody's behind it. The Jew—"

"Stop this nonsense about the Jew!" He twisted Willi's collar. "Who told you to get me down here?"

"Nobody, I swear on my honor!"

"Your honor—" Feller shoved Willi back contemptuously. "God knows who's behind this. I'll have a talk with Jähde tomorrow morning. He'll clear things up."

144

The block leader was calming down.

"If you do that," said Willi, "we'll never catch the Jew."

Feller wasn't listening. He began to shine his light around the pantry systematically. He counted the jars and the remaining sausages and checked the contents of the sacks and bags. He couldn't keep his mouth from watering.

"I'll take the provisions for safekeeping," Feller said.

Willi said nothing.

"You can help me carry the things home."

"Now?" Willi asked in surprise. "You can do that during the day!"

"Tomorrow I won't have time for things like that," Feller said quickly. "If you behave wisely now, I'll think twice about talking to Jähde."

Willi looked skeptically at the block leader. What did the provisions have to do with the Jew? Or did Feller just want them himself?

"What do you mean, wisely?" Willi asked warily.

"I can prove that you lied to me in my capacity as block leader and that you dragged me here by night. Did you know there were provisions here?"

"No," Willi lied.

"That's the only thing I believe. You couldn't be so stupid." Feller laughed. "You would have eaten them yourself!"

Willi wanted to speak.

"Come on, load up as much as you can carry."

The block leader took the slab of ham from its nail.

"I'll have the public soup kitchen pick up the rest tomorrow," he said, and the smell of smoked meat teased his nostrils.

14

ABIRAM AND THE THREE FRIENDS had left the cellar. Antek hit on the idea of hiding Abiram for the time being in one of the little towers at the town gate. It would be cramped, but if he had to he could sleep there. A tiny spiral staircase led to the small round room at the top of the tower above the sentry's passageway along the wall. The loopholes almost at ground level allowed a view of both sides of the gate. That was advantageous. They took enough provisions along so that Abiram would have enough to eat for the next few days.

Since there was just enough space in the little tower room for Abiram to lie down, they stacked cans and jars in the passageway above the gate. Zick hung the sausages on bricks that jutted out on the inner side of the shadowed wall.

"It looks like the land of milk and honey," Abiram smiled. He had lost all his fear.

It was cold, and the wind blew through their light jackets. Abiram draped the Army jacket around Zick's shoulders.

"Tomorrow I'll bring you something else to wear,"

Antek said. "We've got to get rid of that jacket. How did Ruth ever come up with the idea of bringing you an Army jacket!"

"She probably wasn't thinking," Abiram tried to excuse her.

"That's just it!"

"Say, don't you want to hear how Paule got the spare key?" Paule asked, offended. He was sitting at the head of the passageway between two crenels, the notches atop the tower. His back was to the fields of rubble. "After all, you owe me your freedom."

"All right, tell us."

"I took a wax impression of Willi's key. The dope didn't even notice, and then I traded my copper pipe for the key. Pretty good, right?"

"And you did that for me?" Abiram asked.

Antek turned around quickly, and Paule started to blush. "The things you ask," he muttered.

Suddenly Paule straightened up. "Shhh!" He shoved himself down from the wall to the opposite side, bent over the edge, and motioned to his friends.

A few yards from the entrance Willi was standing with a man. They must have heard something, because they were rooted to the spot. Then the man said something to Willi and both of them went on through the gate toward Schiller Street.

"That lousy pig!" Paule hissed.

"Go on now," Abiram said when Willi and the man were out of hearing range. "When Willi comes back, you've got to be back at school. Then he'll have a hard time proving anything on you."

"And what about you?" asked Antek.

"You've helped me enough." He pointed to the cans

and sausages. "I can last here until the Russians come!"

"What, you're waiting for the Russians? You've got a screw loose. What do you think you'll get from them?"

"Freedom," Abiram said simply.

"Freedom," Paule tapped his finger against his forehead. "Ask the refugees, they'll tell you about freedom!"

"The Russians castrate everybody," said Zick, and a shiver ran down his spine.

"So, they castrate people? Do you even know what that means?" Antek asked.

"Well, anyway, it's something that's very unpleasant for men and women," Zick spat back.

Paule doubled over with enjoyment. "Zick, that's your best joke yet!"

"Forget it, Zick," Abiram said, "it's certainly unpleasant, only the Russians won't do it to us."

Antek looked at his watch. "Well, what shall we do with you now?" he asked Abiram. "I don't think it's the brightest idea in the world either, to wait here for the Russians. Where were you heading when you came to this town?"

"Oh, there's no sense in that," Abiram said, declining to answer Antek's question.

"Tell us, maybe we can help you!"

Abiram shook his head. "No, you can't. You'll only put yourselves in danger."

"You're making too big a deal of it, you can spare us your mother-hen concern about it!" Paule said rudely.

"All right, I was looking for a man named Arthur Dressler, who's supposed to live here. I don't know him either. A man in the camp slipped me his address. For months I've been living on addresses like that. Sometimes it works out well, sometimes it doesn't."

"Good," Antek interrupted, "at least we'll find out where he lives, what he's doing, and whether he knows of a safe hiding place for you."

With that the three boys left Abiram in order to be back at the school before Willi. He might return at any moment from his unsuccessful attempt to have them arrested.

On the way home Antek asked, "Paule, why did you make a duplicate key?"

"Will you tell me why you arranged with Ruth that she should help Abiram without telling us about it?" Paule asked back.

Both boys were silent until they reached the school. Once more they succeeded in creeping through the corridors unnoticed until they reached their beds. Willi was not back yet. They slipped under their covers, greatly relieved.

None of them knew how much time had gone by when they heard the door open. Even Zick wasn't yet asleep. The thick blackout paper on the windows blocked the moonlight out completely. They sensed Willi pushing himself through the door. Paule made an effort to breathe regularly. Willi felt his way to the light switch and snapped the night light on. Antek saw Willi bend over Zick's bed and look thoughtfully into his face.

It wasn't easy for Zick to lie motionless. He felt Willi's gaze. His hands were sweating under the covers. What should he say if Willi were to wake him up now? Zick's eyeballs rolled under closed lids. Get away from me, get away from me, he thought over and over, and then Willi did turn around and go to look at Paule, who was also lying still, pretending to be asleep.

"You're not sleeping," said Willi.

Paule kept on breathing calmly. He even managed to insert a rattling snore every now and then.

When Willi came to Antek's bed, he saw Antek looking at him and was startled.

"Where did you put the Jew?"

"I don't know what you're talking about," said Antek in a friendly voice. "Go to bed, Willi, you're already dreaming!"

"Stop it, I'm warning you! How did you get out of the cellar and where did you put the Jew?" He shook Paule.

"Don't wake me up, you idiot," Paule said in a wide-awake voice. "I don't know any Jew. If you keep on making so much noise, Nagold will come and you can tell him your story about a Jew."

Now Willi saw what the boys had planned for him. "You're not going to get off that easily," he hissed and pulled the covers off Zick. "Will you tell me now what's going on?"

Zick gathered his courage. "You're crazy," he peeped. "Why do you have your gym suit and a sweater on in the middle of the night? Are you cold?"

Then Willi began to hit him.

"Always hit people littler than you," Antek said calmly.

The way his friends were pretending not to know what he was talking about was making Willi furious. He was forced to realize that he could prove nothing against them. He shone the flashlight into their faces.

The three friends smiled at him.

"Willi," said Antek, his voice full of concern, "go to bed and get some sleep. You seem to be having a wild nightmare."

"You'll pay for this," Willi stammered. He rolled himself up in his blanket and bawled with rage.

Willi found out nothing about Abiram the next morning, either. Antek, Paule, and Zick shrugged their shoulders uncomprehendingly.

"We really don't know what you're talking about," was their invariable answer. Threats, pleas, and anger had no effect on them. There was nothing left for Willi to do but to look for the Jew on his own.

But neither Willi nor Antek were able to carry out their plans. The caravans started off at first light. Until well into the morning all the streets of the town were jammed. Several extra helpers were needed to divert the caravans into side streets so as to avoid chaos at the main crossings. Antek was charged with supervising the entry of the refugees along the main street. It was not an easy job. The people were nervous, tired, and anxious. They wanted to take the shortest path through town and not squeeze through the narrow side streets of the old part of town in their overloaded wagons. A traffic jam—they had been through worse things. Anyone who didn't make it through could just lie where he fell. There was no courtesy or consideration. All that mattered was time.

Antek stood on the street with extended arms, the yoke of a horse team pushing against him.

"Move out of the way or I'll run you down," a farmer shouted. "We'll find our way ourselves!"

Antek grabbed the reins and turned the horse to the left.

"If you want to get through town and go farther west, then you've got to bear left!"

From between the two horses he saw the farmer raise his whip. "I know better than that!"

Someone tore the whip from the farmer's hand. "Come on, drive to the left! Don't you see what's going on there by the church? People can't move forward or backward. The boy is right, he's giving us good directions!"

Cursing, the farmer turned left into the side street.

Antek wiped the sweat from his forehead. The leaders of a caravan were always the hardest to direct, the other wagons seldom went off on their own, they followed their bellwether like sheep. Antek's job was to keep the wagons going to the left until the market square was relatively empty, and then the wagons would be directed into the side streets to the right. If they could keep to this schedule of rotation, there would be almost no crush of traffic within the town.

Antek saw Ruth standing across the street in an entryway. She waved. Antek turned his back on her. After everything that had happened, he had nothing more to say to her. It had all started with her showing off by playing the sympathetic one with the Jew while he and his friends looked like villains. Later she had secretly tried to help the Jew. And finally she hadn't come yesterday evening.

Antek sneaked a look across the street. She was leaning against the wall. It looked as if she wanted to tell him something. He didn't care. Let her stand till she turned black.

Antek raised his arm. It was time to change the direction of traffic. The wagons were now driving so that they blocked Ruth's view of him. Then he remembered Willi. What would happen if he started

asking questions of Ruth? How could she know what
had happened last night and that all of them had to
deny Abiram's existence to Willi? In his own anger,
Antek had forgotten that danger. He bent down to look
under a wagon and across to Ruth. He couldn't leave
his post. The people would immediately start veering
off right and left at random just to get somewhere.

The only thing he could do was give the owl signal,
she would have to hear that.

Antek put his hands to his mouth. He looked around
uncertainly, a traffic policeman who had just been
assertively directing the refugees on their way, now
imitating the drawn-out cry of an owl. A girl who was
sitting backwards on a wagon called out as she passed:
"The Russians must have stolen your brains!"

Antek felt horribly silly.

But Ruth had heard the call. Because the line of
wagons had paused at that moment, she crawled
through between a horse and the axle of a wagon.

"I have to tell you why I couldn't come last night,"
she started without preliminaries and told about her
experience with the woman and the baby.

Antek listened without saying anything.

"Don't you understand why I had to stay?" she asked
impatiently.

Antek raised his arm and pointed to the right. Ruth
was pushed and jostled around.

"Maybe," he finally answered when it had become
quieter.

"But that doesn't matter now. You went off and
acted on your own and that's why Abiram has to get out
of here now. Willi reported him."

"No!" Ruth grabbed Antek's arm.

"Don't make a scene!"

"Where is he now, what's happened?"

"You've done enough harm with your Army jacket. We won't tell you his hiding place a second time."

"You can't do that," Ruth said softly, "I was just trying to help him. I couldn't know that the soldier would leave me like that."

"You did it without me," said Antek still more softly.

His coldness wounded her. She turned and walked away.

"Stay here," Antek said. "If Willi comes looking for you, avoid him, get it?"

"And you want me to do nothing for Abiram?"

"I didn't say that. I just don't want you to know where he's hidden. Because you'll do something stupid again!"

"You're jealous!"

"Jealous of you?" He was furious that she had seen through him. "Of you, because of a—" Antek was just barely able to swallow the last word. "You're not really that important to me."

"Then tell me what I can do for him!"

Antek considered it for a while. "Try to find out where a man by the name of Arthur Dressler lives. But be careful, and don't say a word to Willi, understand?"

Ruth nodded and ran past the caravan wagons to the market, turned around once more, and Antek could just make out her smile.

Paule had succeeded in escaping for a short while from the duty assigned by Jähde. As he pushed past people and wagons and watched Antek directing traffic for a while, he considered how he could best conduct the search for Arthur Dressler. At the edge of town he happened to find himself in a line of people waiting to

154

make purchases. He let himself be shoved slowly forward. There were potatoes, the only food that was still available anywhere.

"You don't have a shopping bag," said a boy behind him, in an unfamiliar dialect, "why are you standing in line?"

Paule turned around. A fourteen-year-old was observing him. "What business is that of yours?" Paule sensed the attention of the people around him. The potato woman came to his aid.

"Take hold of this," she called to him. Her crate was empty, and she wanted Paule to reach down several sacks of potatoes from the wagon standing behind them.

"That's a gentleman," the potato woman said kindly.

Paule smiled. "Oh, I'm glad to help," he said, and then he added softly, "do you know if there's an Arthur Dressler living in the neighborhood?"

The face of the woman, friendly a moment ago, became still. She pulled Paule close.

"I'm no information bureau, my boy, get out of here as fast as your legs can carry you. And don't let me catch sight of you again!"

She dragged her sack back to the table herself.

"What times we're living in," she muttered as she filled a shopping bag someone held out to her.

Paule left. He didn't understand the woman's behavior, but it seemed the name Dressler spelled trouble.

He hadn't gone far when he heard steps behind him. The fourteen-year-old boy stood there.

"Who are you looking for?" he asked.

"Why?" Paule responded.

"I have connections. I know a lot. For a couple of

155

cigarettes . . ." The boy stretched out his dirty hand.

"I'll shove a couple of cigarettes in your face!" Paule walked away from him. It started to rain. Paule pulled his jacket over his head. To be traveling on the highways now must be awful.

He watched sympathetically as two women dragged a loaded child's wagon along by a strap over their shoulders. The springs had broken and had been laboriously tied together with string. Who knew how many weeks they had been traveling.

Then Paule saw the pastor. "He ought to know," he thought, went up to him, and greeted him. The pastor returned his greeting. It wasn't easy for Paule to start a conversation with the pastor on the street in the rain.

"Sir, could I ask you something?"

"Of course, my son. Do you want to come to the rectory with me?"

"Thank you, but that's not necessary," Paule declined. "I just wanted to know if you know a man named Arthur Dressler and where he lives."

Paule waited anxiously. But just as with the potato woman, he met a strange resistance from the pastor.

"Why do you want to know that?"

Paule was prepared for this question. "Some refugees passing through asked me to give him their greetings. They didn't know his address but they wanted to get a message to him."

"Oh?" said the pastor. Paule felt very uncomfortable.

"My son," the pastor said as he walked slowly beside Paule down the street. His pointed black shoes squirted water with each step. "I have forgotten this man's address."

Paule had been watching the pastor's splattering

156

shoes. Now he raised his head in astonishment. But the pastor made no move to explain himself.

"Forgotten?" Paule asked as if he hadn't heard.

"Yes," the pastor said, "this man turned away from God. But I have to give myself to those who seek the grace of God and the church in order to find consolation and strength therein."

"But these people wanted to give him a message!" Paule tried again.

"I tell you, I've forgotten it." The pastor stopped walking. "In any case," he closed the subject, "if I knew it I wouldn't tell you. God bless you!" And Paule was dismissed.

Jähde had been pleased to see that Antek's crossing had the best regulated flow of traffic. He clapped the boy on the shoulder. "I like what you're doing. Do you think you can handle it this afternoon, too, when there'll be a bigger crush of refugees for a while?"

"Yes, sir," Antek answered, standing at attention.

"Well, well, we're making something of you after all!"

Antek felt that time was pressing. He wanted to look for Dressler. And he would have liked to exchange Abiram's army jacket while it was raining.

"Could I be relieved now, so that I can come back and work this afternoon?"

Jähde had no objection to that, since the caravans had thinned out for the moment.

"Look over there," Jähde said and pointed across the square to Kimmich, who was just in the process of helping a young woman with her baby. "Even your music master is involved!"

Kimmich had seen Jähde, too, and it made him uncomfortable to see how familiarly he was treating Antek. He saw Jähde clap Antek on the shoulder.

"I thank you and your granddaughter with all my heart," the young woman was saying.

Kimmich nodded. His thoughts were on Jähde. He remembered how angry Antek had been when he left Kimmich's apartment. "No," Antek had said as he ran out, "I understand nothing!"

If Antek had told Jähde about their conversation yesterday, that could be very bad for Kimmich.

Antek had not let Kimmich out of his sight. Kimmich was the right person to ask about Dressler. Antek wanted to talk about Abiram and what would happen to him. But that would be a new danger for Kimmich, and the connection with a former prisoner could be a burden on Abiram, too.

Antek caught up with Kimmich behind the granary. "Mr. Kimmich," he called.

Kimmich was startled to see Antek suddenly before him.

"I'd like to ask you something."

"Yes, what is it?"

The sudden friendliness after the equally friendly talk between Antek and Jähde made Kimmich skeptical. He looked warily at Antek, who didn't notice his suspicion.

"I'm looking for Arthur Dressler," Antek said, and after some hesitation he added, "after our conversation yesterday I thought that you might know his address."

The way Antek brought out his question strengthened Kimmich's suspicions. Jähde had set the boy on him as a spy, and it was only Antek's inexperience that allowed Kimmich to see through him so quickly.

"No," Kimmich answered, "I've never heard the name."

"You really haven't? I mean, I thought he could be someone who was politically . . ." Antek didn't know how to proceed. "Well, who might have the same political opinions as you. You must know someone like that in this town."

"That's enough, Antek. Or else I'll lose control of myself. One thing is clear to me: I trusted you too much yesterday. Too bad!"

Kimmich crossed the street in the direction of his apartment. Antek felt deep disappointment. Who can I rely on now? he thought. He felt he was living in a world full of hatred, suspicion, and lies. He wanted to make it up! Kimmich's words came back to him again. But make it up to whom, and how, and why?

Antek and Paule had forbidden Zick to look for Dressler. "You'll open your mouth and all of a sudden out will come Abiram's name or something." That had been the end of it.

While the older boys were busy helping to direct traffic, the younger ones helped in the school building. After the last refugees had left their quarters, the classrooms and halls had to be cleaned for the coming night. Trash and garbage were collected in a bucket, Jähde even demanded that they wash everything down with disinfectant.

Zick had arranged it so that he was together with several other boys, because Willi wasn't letting him out of his sight. "I'll get it out of you!" he whispered as he passed.

159

"What does he want with you?" one of the boys asked.

"Oh," Zick made a dismissive gesture. "He's been having bad dreams and now he keeps wanting me to tell him what he said."

Zick gathered garbage. "Listen," he turned to one of the boys when Willi had gone, "if you come to a town where you don't know anybody and you're looking for someone, what do you do?"

"You go to the registry office, of course," said the boy, "unless it's been closed or the people have taken off."

Zick nodded thoughtfully. "Not bad!"

The rain had stopped by the time Zick ran to the town hall. He was certain no one had thought to ask about Dressler there.

In the foyer of the building Zick read the roster. There it was: Mezzanine—Registry Office, Room 3, Local Group Leader, Room 4. He buttoned up his shirt collar and pulled up his knee socks. Then he knocked. No one answered. Zick took the silence as an invitation to enter Room 3.

A large, stuffy room. Most of the documents had been pulled off the shelves and lay scattered in disordered heaps on the ground. Now Zick noticed that the iron stove in the corner was giving off an unusual amount of heat. We haven't had coal all year, he thought, puzzled, and they're heating here in April as if it were Christmas.

A girl with a red face was digging through the papers. She tore several pages out of a binder without opening the rings.

"Here it is!" she called to the open door of the adjoining room.

"Then burn it with the other documents," came the answer.

The girl stood up, groaning.

Zick cleared his throat. "Heil Hitler!"

The girl dropped the poker in fright.

I'd like to know what she's doing, thought Zick and stood on tiptoes. "I'd like some information, please."

The girl came closer. "Can't you knock?"

Zick looked right into her nostrils, which were black with dust and the ashes of paper.

"I did!"

"What do you want?"

"Could you please give me the address of Arthur Dressler?"

The girl opened her eyes wide.

"Wait a minute," she said and backed towards the door from which the other voice had come.

The local group leader appeared. "Heil Hitler!" Zick greeted him and clicked his heels together.

"What's your name?" asked the official.

Zick found the man to be very friendly.

"Siegfried Breuner."

"Where do you live?"

"I'm a student at the boarding school."

"Do you know who I am?"

"Yes, sir, Group Leader!"

Zick clicked his heels together once more. You never knew.

The local group leader looked at him for a long time with no expression at all.

"And you are looking for Arthur Dressler?"

Zick nodded.

The heat in the room was becoming unbearable.

"Who sent you here?" the official suddenly roared.

With one jump Zick was at the door and flitted out into the hall.

"We'll get to the bottom of this," said the group leader.

He went to the telephone and called Jähde. He demanded an investigation into why students from the boarding school were asking about the Communist Arthur Dressler. Moreover, he demanded, as local group leader, not to be bothered by Jähde's students. "Or," the official concluded in a rage, "maybe you think I've stashed Dressler away at my house to have an alibi for the Russians! Be careful how you treat me!" He slammed the receiver down.

15

RUTH HADN'T YET made any attempt to find Dressler. The thought of not knowing where Abiram was gave her no peace. She wandered around at random, crawled into cellars, peeked into crannies, shoved her way among refugees at the assembly point and in the public soup kitchens, but she couldn't discover a trace of Abiram. She had to find him. She had to make him understand that her grandfather was the only person who could help him now. Then she realized that Antek had not asked her about the Army jacket. Maybe it was still in the cellar. But there was nothing there, not among the cleared shelves or behind the zinc tub or in the crate. But Ruth did discover something else there. A star of David was scratched into the inside of the crate. Ruth pulled it by the lid into the light. She found a piece of iron with which she battered the wood until it broke into pieces.

Not far from Ruth, Willi crept out from behind a pile of rubbish. That noise could only come from the Jew, he thought. Then he discovered Ruth. "What are you doing here?" he shouted. He took his anger at his newest failure out on Ruth.

Ruth didn't know what to say.

"Answer!" Willi bellowed. Ruth shook her head.

"I don't hit girls," said Willi. He stared angrily at her hair, which had escaped from its braid.

Ruth began to plait it together again.

"I don't discuss things with girls either!"

Ruth shrugged her shoulders.

"Sit down over there!"

Ruth sat down hesitantly where he had pointed. Willi sat down next to her.

"What were you doing here?"

"Kindling wood."

"Where were you yesterday?"

"At home. There was a sick woman at our house."

"Where did the boys hide the Jew?"

"I don't know!"

Willi grabbed her wrist.

"Did you talk to Antek?"

"Yesterday," Ruth said without trying to defend herself.

He let her go.

Ruth rubbed the red place above her wrist. "Why are you doing this?" she asked.

Willi's foot kicked against a piece of wood. "I told you, I don't discuss things with girls, any more than I hit them. I have other ways."

He crouched down in front of Ruth. "If you don't tell me right away, I'll go to Jähde!"

"So what?"

"You wait," Willi clicked his tongue, "I'll tell Jähde that what happened the other day with your grandfather's motet was no accident, that he taught it to Paule and Antek."

"You can't do that!" she whispered.

"Yes I can, unless you tell me where the Jew is . . ." Willi waited patiently. "That could mean prison for your grandfather," he added lazily. "And all for a dirty Jew . . ."

Ruth jumped up. "But I don't know anything! Even if I wanted to I couldn't tell you anything. Besides, that doesn't have anything to do with Grandfather!"

"That's my business!"

Willi thought it over. Maybe the boys hadn't told Ruth where they had hidden the Jew. "Good," he said, "if you don't know where he's hidden, it's enough if you come to the block leader with me or even to Jähde and tell that you saw a Jew named Abiram with your own eyes yesterday here in the cellar and that you saw me lock him up."

Ruth turned pale. "No, I can't do that!"

"Then I'll go after your grandfather. You have to figure out who you care more about!" Willi laughed. Now he knew he'd won. "I don't know why you're making such a fuss! The Jew won't overthrow the labor camp they'll put him in."

Then Ruth jumped at Willi. She hit him, scratched, and kicked him. "You dirty beast," she shouted, "you rat!"

Willi was unprepared for her attack, and he stumbled and slipped.

Ruth ran away. She heard Willi's threatening calls and ran as fast as she could. She tore her skirt on a jagged piece of metal. She heard Willi behind her. Now she was close to the town gate. With one leap she dove into a crater half filled with rubbish. She lay stretched out on her stomach, her face pressed into the grass. She heard Willi's footsteps as he raced right by the crater. He hadn't seen her.

Cautiously Ruth sat up. With great difficulty she clambered out of the hole, and then—Ruth pressed her hands to her mouth. Abiram's head had appeared at one of the loopholes in the town gate.

Ruth hadn't been mistaken. Willi must have seen him too. Now everyone was lost, Abiram, her grandfather, and Antek.

Once Ruth was home, it was hard for Kimmich to get a coherent account from her. She burst out crying again and again.

"He wants to turn you in, Grandfather!"

"There's nothing to turn me in for. Jähde already came to see me about the motet." He pulled Ruth close.

"Does Willi know anything about Dressler?"

She shook her head.

"Who knows about Dressler?"

"Antek, Paule, Zick, and I. The boys wanted to find him for Abiram."

"And you saw Abiram in the gate tower?"

"Yes!"

"You stay here now," said Kimmich. "And lock the door after me. Don't open for anyone until I get back."

The telephone conversation with the local group leader had shown Jähde that his suspicions about Kimmich were justified. He paid no attention to the personal remarks of the group leader. He ascribed them to the general overwrought state caused by the temporary crisis at the front. He, Jähde, would keep his head. He saw his duty more clearly than ever: he had to be vigilant here at home and foil the plans of people like Kimmich and friends.

Jähde closed himself in his office. He didn't want to be disturbed. He had to plan how to set a trap for Kimmich, Dressler, and others of their persuasion. He had to find out from the boys which of them Kimmich had been using as a bloodhound.

The windowpanes rattled in the thunder of the artillery. Since morning the rumble of the guns had come closer. More and more soldiers were seen among the refugees. But Jähde didn't notice that—he didn't want to notice it.

There was a knock at the door.

Paule asked if they would be singing vespers in the church.

"Of course, or is Mr. Nagold afraid?" Jähde threw his pencil down on his desk in anger.

"I don't think so," Paule said, "it's just because of how close the front is."

"Who told you that?" Jähde interrupted him. "Send him to me, your Mr. Nagold. I would like to share my opinion with him. Anyway, you will sing vespers and you'll wear your choir outfits as usual!"

"Yes sir!" Paule adopted military posture and went. He ran into Zick, who was hanging around in front of the door.

"What are you doing here?"

"Nothing." Zick blushed.

Paule bent over to the smaller boy. "I didn't find anything out. Not even from the pastor. He just talked nonsense. What about you?"

Zick avoided Paule's eyes. "I didn't either."

Now Paule was becoming suspicious. "What's the

matter with you? Did you give us away?"

"No, I didn't."

"Well then, go and change. Jähde said we're going to sing. I'm supposed to get Nagold."

"Does Jähde want to see him?" Zick was beginning to suspect something.

"Yes, there must be trouble!" Paule left Zick and went to find Nagold.

Nagold had stretched out, exhausted, on his bed. The previous day he and the boys had rearranged the school furnishings to make room for the refugees. That had overtaxed his strength. During the night he had hardly slept. An old man had died. No one knew his name or who his people were, people had just called him "Grandpa." The pastor and Nagold had carried him out of the school and taken him in a wheelbarrow to the cemetery. There were already many graves there marked only by a hastily erected wooden cross.

The next morning the three hundred refugees had to be directed to their caravans again. The building was prepared for the arrival of new refugees.

Now, this afternoon, Nagold was longing for sleep.

"You haven't eaten anything yet today," Mrs. Nagold said. She sat stiffly on her chair, her hands folded in her lap, and looked over at him. She wanted him to speak and to look at her.

"No," he said, motionless.

Mrs. Nagold shifted closer.

Nagold creased his forehead. Why couldn't she leave him alone! He could feel that she wanted consolation from him. But her obtrusiveness repelled him. Had she still not seen that he had become indifferent to the world around him and that he no longer felt any kind of responsibility? He felt her cold fingers on the back of his hand.

"I have some soup. That'll do you good!"

When he neither answered nor looked at her, she continued: "We don't have any food for tomorrow. I've used the last of the flour."

"Then cook potatoes! But for God's sake leave me alone!"

But she slid from her chair and knelt beside his bed, put her face into his hands and whispered: "Don't leave me alone. You're the only human being I'm living for."

When he felt her timid kisses on the palms of his hands, he balled his fingers into a fist.

Mrs. Nagold got up without a word. He didn't know whether she felt his distaste. He heard her busying herself at the stove, and soon he smelled the stale odor of cabbage soup. He was hungry.

As Nagold was silently spooning his soup, Paule came with the news that Nagold was wanted by Jähde right away.

Zick stood at the keyhole and didn't know whether to put his ear or his eye to the narrow opening. He didn't get to see much: a hand, a leg, a back, or Jähde's face.

"What's the idea of canceling vespers?" Jähde asked Nagold without greeting.

"I think there are more important things to do!" Nagold responded.

"You leave the thinking to me. I want the choir to sing. I want to avoid anything that might set off a panic. For decades there's been a choir singing at vespers on Friday afternoons, so there will be today too. Do you understand?" Zick saw Nagold bend his head. But Jähde's outstretched hand cut off his view.

"Then there's another thing. Zick was at the registry office today. He was trying in the most ridiculous way to ask about Arthur Dressler. Do you know who that is?"

Zick didn't hear any more. He ran off in a panic.

"Isn't that the man who was released from the labor camp with Kimmich?"

"Right. But there's a warrant out for this man's arrest again, for subversion. Kimmich is in it with him, and the fact that Zick was asking about Dressler at the local group leader's office is proof that now Kimmich is involving my students in his filthy business. Yesterday it was the motet, today this! Doesn't it seem strange to you?"

Nagold didn't understand Jähde's talk about Kimmich and his influence on the children. "If Kimmich wanted to use the boys to get in touch with this Dressler, then he certainly wouldn't send Zick to the local group leader to ask for the address. That doesn't make sense."

"I didn't ask you if it made sense, Nagold. You have a talent for putting important things in such a way that they seem trivial. That doesn't show you in a good light!"

Nagold's face closed up. Let Jähde do whatever he wanted. He saw no cause to get involved in something whose senselessness was clear from the very beginning.

"I want to interrogate the boys. And I want you to be there."

"What do I have to do with it?"

"That's what I mean to find out!"

It took a while to convince Jähde that an interrogation, as he had put it, was impossible before vespers. How were the children supposed to sing and maintain discipline when Jähde had just told them they were suspected of being spies? Finally Jähde agreed to talk with the boys after the singing in the church.

Zick had run to find his friends. They had changed clothes and were standing in their dark pants and white shirts in front of the school, waiting to go to the church. Word had gotten around among the strangers that the boys' choir would sing for vespers in the church as usual. Maybe it would be the last time.

Zick pulled Paule and Antek aside. Antek made a negative gesture. "Not here! Let's get farther away."

They went into the long unused cloister, where they felt no one could watch them.

"All right, tell!" Antek commanded.

"I went to the registry office today to ask about Dressler," Zick began, breathless.

"Registry office," Paule sighed and made a face.

"Go on!" Antek said.

"Nothing else. The local group leader asked who sent me."

"Oh, you went right to him?" Paule clapped his hands.

"He wanted to tell Jähde about it," Zick wailed, "and I listened at the door."

Paule nodded. "That's why you were creeping around there just now!"

"What did you hear?" Antek asked.

"Nagold was supposed to tell Jähde why I was asking about Dressler. Jähde was really angry."

Zick looked at his friends anxiously. "Does Jähde

already know about Abiram? Maybe Willi told, or Ruth?"

"Nonsense," said Antek.

The bells began to peal and drowned out their words.

"I'm going to run to the town gate and warn Abiram," Paule screeched over the bells. "If Nagold asks about me, find some excuse, I'm in the toilet or I'm throwing up, anything. If I find Abiram, then everything's all right. If not, then something must have happened."

Paule flew down the cloister corridor. His heels clicked on the tiles, and as he jumped over the prayer benches Antek involuntarily ducked his head. Zick made the sign of the cross on his chest.

Nagold crossed the square with the students. Zick and Antek fell in with them unobtrusively. Quietly they entered the church and walked up to the organ. The light inside was dim, most of the windowpanes of the church had been broken and repaired with cardboard. Nagold had them light candles and noticed that Paule was missing. He looked a question at Antek.

"He's coming in a minute. He wasn't feeling well."

Antek whispered so that he couldn't be heard in the nave of the church. Nagold put Zick in Paule's place.

Paule reached the town gate, panted up the spiral stairs to the little tower—it was empty.

Paule called out, no answer.

The shards of several jars of preserves lay forlorn in the sentry's passageway.

Zick was right, Abiram had been captured.

Paule stumbled back down the stairs and chased back to the church as fast as he had come.

He could hear the choir from a distance. They were

singing the piece in which he had a solo. He cautiously pushed down the heavy handle of the church door. As he silently climbed the wooden stairs, he had to hold on to the railing. The boys' voices resounded through the nave:

> Cruel death the archer, grim and stark,
> His aim is always true,
> His arrows fly straight to the mark,
> There's no escape for you.
> Life disappears like smoke in wind,
> No living thing escapes,
> Your treasures you must leave behind,
> He'll take you from this place.

Paule had never grasped the sense of the words so clearly as today. Suddenly he was seized by the desire to sing his solo. His breath came quickly and his voice broke. But then it gained in strength as Paule closed his eyes to hide his tears.

> Today could be your last on earth,
> Your life's last, closing day.
> Pay careful heed, I speak the truth:
> Let virtue guide your way . . .

The congregation sat with folded hands, moved by the song about their own fate.

"Today could be your last on earth." For Nagold there was no maybe about it. It was his last day. His goodbye to music, to his church, and to his students. What was left for him was a wandering with no goal and no faith.

16

ABIRAM HAD LAIN shivering but happy in the drafty tower above the gate just as Paule, Antek, and Zick had left him. After the friends had disappeared in the darkness, he had tried to find a position that would let him survey the town and the fields of ruins from the loopholes. The floor was hard, and only his head was cushioned on the Army jacket. When he looked through the western loophole all he could see in the moonlight was rubble, ruined chimneys, and rusty iron bars and mesh. His eyes wandered tiredly over the ruins of Schiller Street. A light flared up and disappeared. Abiram knew they were looking for him. They were shining lights into every cranny, they were climbing every pile of stones, no cellar was too deep for them to find him. The eastern loophole gave him a view of the town. The church tower loomed up in the night-blue sky. Abiram thought about what people could be praying for in this church that was so strange to him.

Suddenly the sky was illuminated by broad reddish-blue flashes. The light that had been looking for him disappeared. And while the townspeople sat anxiously in their houses and counted the seconds between the

174

flashes and the thunder of artillery, Abiram found peace and hope again. He stretched out and slept through the unceasing explosions.

By day it was not easy for Abiram to remain unnoticed in the town gate. The slightest movement brought the danger that he could be seen. He could be in the passageway only if he crawled or lay down, and in the tower he could only sit if he pulled his legs up tight. So for the most part he lay out in the passageway on his back. But he ate without stopping. He couldn't remember ever in his life having had such a wide choice of things to eat. He didn't even need to move. He reached out to the left, to the right, or above him where the sausages were hanging, kept his patience, and was happy.

It started to rain. Abiram crept back into the little tower. He wondered whether one of the boys had found Dressler. Maybe the man no longer lived here! Suddenly he heard steps and someone called close by. He put his face up to the loophole—he saw Willi on the path between the ruins. Funny, he had thought the steps were much closer. Abiram scooted back again. All his patience, all his happiness about his new friends had disappeared. All that was left was suspicion and vigilance.

Abiram didn't know how long he had crouched in his corner. Maybe one hour, maybe two. But then he saw a man with white hair walking purposefully toward the town gate. Abiram pulled himself farther back. With feverish speed he rolled up the Army jacket with its lining out. The man must be right under him in the gate by now. He seemed to be undecided. Abiram crept to the passageway. But he couldn't see the man. Had he climbed up to one of the towers? Abiram didn't know to which one. He leaned out over the crenels. It was impossible to jump down.

Now the tapping on the steps was clearly audible. It was coming from the right. Abiram fled, almost doubled over, along the passageway to the left tower. He stopped in the middle. What was that? Was his hearing playing tricks on him, or was the man coming up the left tower? Abiram's hands went to his throat. He was trapped.

"Abiram?"

The voice came from the left. Abiram had to get back to the other side. But was there a stairway there that led down?

"Abiram, stop! Don't be afraid!"

The man appeared. He was dusty and covered with whitewash, because the stairway was very narrow.

Abiram ducked down and knocked over two jars full of cherry preserves. The glass splintered with a crash on the stones.

"Stop, boy!"

But Abiram was already at the other side of the gate. He crept into the tower. His hands felt around on the door that led down, but they found no latch.

The man was coming closer.

Abiram leaned out of the loophole that looked to the north. The town wall was two yards beneath him. Abiram pressed the Army jacket together, tucked it under his chin, and slid backwards out of the loophole. He hung for a moment in the air, hanging on to the wall with just his hands.

He saw the white-haired man's head appear.

He let himself drop.

His feet landed neatly on the narrow wall. Abiram balanced along it until he reached the upper branches of a chestnut tree growing next to it. He hid himself from the man among the leaves.

Now he crept along the town wall, over fences and through gardens, until he came to the grounds of a small factory. There was an open yard in front of him. Pipes were fastened on the wall of the factory, and on the other side of the yard were barrels. They were numbered with white oil paint. Abiram was disturbed by a small wooden hut that stood in the middle of the yard. It had windows on all four sides and he couldn't tell whether there was someone inside or not.

To Abiram's left was the town wall, which he couldn't scale. To his right were buildings. Courtyards and gardens were sealed off by gratings. The sky was darkening. Should he wait here until evening? Abiram thought about the man who had been after him. He took a stone and threw it across the factory yard until it rolled against a barrel. Nothing stirred. Abiram climbed over the wire fence. The windowpanes stared at him like huge telescopes, and it took all his self-control not to bolt and flee. The gravel crunched under his feet. There were ten of these numbered barrels at regular intervals between Abiram and the hut he had to pass. Abiram had reached the first barrel. He ducked down and waited, but all he could hear was the pounding of his own heart. Then he came up behind the second barrel, the third, the fourth.

From here he could see the entrance to the hut. In its open door lay a German shepherd. It was lying with its muzzle on its paws, across the threshold. Its amber eyes had long since caught sight of Abiram. Silently alert, the dog followed his every move. In the hut sat an old man, sleeping.

Abiram crept to the fifth barrel. The dog inched forward on its belly. It didn't growl and it didn't bark. When Abiram reached the sixth barrel, it lifted its head and its hackles began to rise.

Abiram pulled a piece of sausage from his pocket. He held it at the level of the dog's eyes so it would catch the scent of the sausage. It was a thin dog.

Abiram came to the seventh barrel. He knew that if he were to turn around now and show the dog his back, the dog would attack him. Abiram crouched down. He placed the sausage on the tips of his fingers and stretched his hand out. The dog remained motionless. Only his tongue licked once over his muzzle.

He's hungry, thought Abiram, and had reached the ninth barrel. There were no more than three yards between him and the dog and the sleeping man. Abiram tossed the sausage toward the dog. The animal jerked its paws. It put its ears back, its nose quivered. The dog stood up.

"Take it!" Abiram whispered.

And the dog began to bark. He leaped at Abiram, who was holding the Army jacket between himself and the animal. Abiram crashed into the barrels. The old man came out the door. "Here, Harro!"

The dog leaped back to its master, the jacket in its jaws.

Abiram was looking down the barrel of a pistol.

The man took the jacket from the dog and looked at it thoughtfully. "You ran away?" he asked.

Abiram said nothing.

"You did the right thing, boy, you can't win a war

with children." He threw the jacket into the hut with a gesture of contempt.

He pointed to the barrels. "Gasoline for our lords and masters for when the Russians arrive." The old man laughed. "The game's over. And now get out of here before someone sees you!"

He motioned grumpily to Abiram as the dog snuffled at the sausage.

At that moment the church bells began to ring. Abiram, who had no idea where to go, fled into the church.

The choir sang the final phrase, and the recessional began. Slowly the congregation stood up from the benches. Abiram was pushed out the door by the flood of churchgoers. He couldn't stay here. Willi could appear at any moment. He ran along the street to the market where a caravan was assembling its members to go to their night's lodgings, and he blended into the crowd of refugees. Maybe that was a way of leaving the town unnoticed tomorrow morning.

He saw a young woman with two children. She was carrying a checkered bedspread on her back in which she had gathered all her possessions.

"Give that to me, I'll carry it for you!" said Abiram. "Why?"

"Because you look tired."

No one had said anything like that to the young woman before. Who cared if someone looked tired? She smiled and set the heavy pack down.

"Don't you have any baggage?"

Abiram threw the pack over his shoulder and almost disappeared under it.

"No," he groaned. The pack was much too heavy.

"And your people?"

"They're gone, I don't know where. I lost them a while ago, in Breslau."

"Breslau, are you from there too?" the young woman asked.

As they slowly pushed forward side by side, they talked about her flight. How they had first traveled by train with a lot of luggage, but then after a hundred miles they had had to get out. Then she put what she valued most in the bedspread and rode a while in a freight train. But then that stopped running too. The tracks had been blown up. Since then she'd been on foot. How long? Many weeks. Who knew how far there was yet to go.

They had come into the vicinity of the boarding school and had to line up single file. Abiram pulled the sack across his back so that his head was barely visible.

"What are they doing here?" he asked the woman.

"They're counting heads for the lodgings. Don't you know about this?"

"I've usually looked for lodgings on my own," Abiram said quickly.

"I can't do that, with the children. But go ahead and stay here tonight, the mass lodgings always have soup or tea."

"Seventy-five, seventy-six, seventy-seven," the sister in charge counted off, and Abiram was the next in line.

"That's all," she called out to a man.

She saw Abiram looking after the young woman. "Do you belong with someone in there?"

"Yes, he's with me," the woman said.

"All right, you can come in," the sister said and walked along beside Abiram.

"Where are we staying?"

"Here, in this big building. There's room, and it's very clean," the sister said kindly. "It's the boarding school for our choir students."

Abiram dropped his pack. He was standing directly in front of the steps to the boarding school.

"That can't be," he muttered.

The sister put her hand on his shoulder in a friendly way. "What's wrong? It's a good place to stay. To judge by the way you look, you haven't had a good place for quite a while!"

"Come on," the woman called, one of her children pulled him by the hand.

"No, I'd like to go somewhere else . . ." he looked around.

The sister was becoming impatient. "You can't have your choice of hotels here. You've been counted in, and you're coming along!"

She loaded the pack onto his back again.

Jähde had begun his interrogation in the choir loft of the church. He detained the four boys who had missed yesterday's rehearsal. Nagold sat down on the organ bench as the boys were made to stand at attention near the balcony railing. The only one who was calm in the face of this interrogation was Willi. The agitation of his former friends hadn't escaped his notice. Everything pointed to the fact that something had gone wrong with their Jew. He knew what he had to say when he was questioned.

Jähde's boots squeaked on the floor tiles. He was letting the boys wait.

"Zick!" he called loudly, and the name echoed from

wall to wall all the way to the altar.

Zick stepped forward one pace. His gaze was on the large cross suspended over the main altar under the dome in the middle of the church.

"Were you at the registry office today?" Jähde's voice thundered.

"Yes," whispered Zick. His word hung there in the empty nave.

"Did you ask the local group leader about a man named Arthur Dressler?"

"Yes."

Zick heard Jähde stop behind him. He must be very close, Zick thought. He raised his shoulders about his ears as his hands grasped the sides of his pants for support.

"And why did you want to know where Dressler is?"

Zick squeezed his eyes shut, drew his head further down, and gave no answer.

"Who sent you there?"

Zick knew what was coming. Before the first blow landed, he turned aside. Jähde's hand landed on the wooden balcony railing. The second and third blows struck him with double force.

"Stop!" cried Paule and Antek.

Only Willi stood still. The name Dressler made a new link in the chain around Abiram. He was silent and wanted to remain silent until he had all the evidence in hand.

Nagold sat leaning forward on the organ bench, his face buried in his hands. He had only one wish, that this farce would be over as quickly as possible.

Jähde grabbed Paule. "Does the truth always have to be beaten out of you?"

He looked at Zick, who was hanging onto the balcony railing and wiping his tear-stained face.

"You speak for him," Jähde said.

Now it was Paule standing at the railing looking down on the crucifix. "We four were in a ruined building in the new section of town yesterday during choir practice," Paule began. "There's a pantry we discovered by accident."

"Pantry?" asked Jähde.

"Yes. We went there whenever we had recess—to eat all we wanted."

Nagold let his hands fall from his face and began to laugh. Jähde was looking for spies, beat Zick in the church, dreamed of arrests, and what did he find out? Salami and marmalade. "Don't you think it would be better to discuss these matters somewhere else?"

"Wait until I'm questioning you!" Jähde responded rudely. "All right, what about this cellar?"

Paule's hands grasped the railing. "That's where we ate yesterday."

"And what does the cellar have to do with Dressler?"

"A great deal," said Antek.

Paule, halfway ready to confess, stepped back. Let Antek say it. Zick bit his knuckles. He admired Antek. Only Willi remained skeptical. He stood among the choir stalls, both arms draped over the top of a bench. He knew that Antek would lie.

"We learned that the pantry belonged to a certain Arthur Dressler," Antek said. He refused to look either at his friends or at Willi. He walked up to Jähde and stood right in front of him.

"After we had eaten all that food, our conscience started to bother us. We wanted to know whose food we had been stealing. That's all, sir!"

Willi removed his arms from the top of the stall thoughtfully. The smile on his face didn't fade when Jähde turned to him as the last boy to be questioned.

"That's easy to check," he said ambiguously.

Jähde took his words to mean that Antek had told the truth. He ordered the boys placed under house arrest. "No dinner for you!"

"There's no dinner for us, either, Mr. Jähde. My wife is out of provisions except for a few potatoes!" Nagold responded. "I'd like to ask you not to lock the children up. You're convinced yourself that this is a minor matter."

"My dear Nagold," Jähde said, looking with contempt at the limping man next to him, "I know how to protect the morals of our homeland, even though I don't always hit the target. You know who Dressler is!"

"Yes, of course, but that has nothing to do with the children," Nagold objected impatiently. "If you place too much importance on minor matters, you'll end up punishing innocent people." The quiet of the church square, without the cries of strangers, without the constant sound of artillery in the distance, made Nagold feel peaceful. He breathed deeply.

"I would gladly sacrifice ten innocent people," said Jähde, "if it will help me catch one guilty one! Remember that. That should be your attitude, too, in our battle for the Führer."

Ten innocent people for one guilty person, Nagold thought. That was a strange measure of justice. It was a matter of fate who survived and who died. He locked the children in their sleeping quarters without looking after them.

Antek, Paule, and Zick lay silent on their beds. They hadn't even bothered to take off their shoes.

"Jähde believed you," said Willi. His glance darted from one to the other. "But for how long?'

"Why didn't you contradict us?" Antek asked, bored. He lay with his head propped on a pillow, his chin against his chest, his feet on the bedspread. "Did you have something like an attack of conscience in your dirty soul?" Antek laughed. "But it doesn't matter now."

Willi sat down on Antek's bed. "It wasn't necessary to expose your miserable lies. In ten minutes at the outside Jähde will be here and will really give it to you!"

"Ten minutes can be a long time if you've got to escape," Paule said. He was lying on his stomach with one side of his face against the pillow.

"He hasn't escaped or you wouldn't have lied. You're not that stupid, Paule!" Willi said in a bored tone.

"Thanks," said Paule, turning to the other side.

Willi got up from Antek's bed and went to stand by the door.

"If you were to tell the truth now," he began softly, and Antek had the feeling that his words contained a plea.

"If you ask me, Willi, then I'll tell you that I don't know the difference between truth and lies any more."

Willi felt they were making fun of him. "Then I'll teach it to you."

"You won't do anything of the sort. You'll leave us in peace now."

The key turned in the lock. The boys sat up, startled.

"There you are," Willi said and was the first to stand before Jähde.

"I know that Dressler never lived on Schiller Street, or did you actually think I wouldn't check your statement?" Jähde looked neither at Antek nor at the other boys, but at his watch instead. "You have three minutes to think it over!"

"That's not necessary," said Willi.

Antek merely drew down the corners of his mouth. "Then it was a mistake, sir. Someone gave us the wrong name," Antek mocked.

"I have something to tell you. May I came with you?" Willi intervened.

Jähde unlocked the door and let him out. The other three remained in the room alone.

"Do you still trust the word of honor of a Hitler Youth member?"

Jähde, who sat nervously drumming on his desk, didn't know how to respond to Willi's high-flown introduction.

"I have to know, sir, if I'm to speak honestly!"

"Since I know you well enough to be sure that you won't tell a lie in the presence of the Führer," Jähde pointed to the wall behind him with his thumb, "I'll believe you!"

"Thank you, sir, you are the only person I can still trust!" Willi blushed.

"Sit down," Jähde answered in a friendly voice.

Willi remained standing. "None of us knows who Dressler is. But there's something else behind this." Willi told Jähde how he had come to sing the motet the other day. That Paule and Antek had known it before and that they had forced him to sight-read the music. Antek was often at Kimmich's and was close friends with his granddaughter.

186

Jähde listened attentively and had begun to take notes when Willi finished his report.

"Go on," Jähde said, "that's nothing so far!"

Willi gathered his strength. "I don't want to tell you anymore now."

"Are you mad? You're forgetting who you're talking to!"

"No, sir. But a moment ago you said you believed the word of honor of a Hitler Youth member. I am one and I give you my word of honor that I can explain everything to you this evening if you release me from house arrest for one hour now!"

"Oh, nonsense, house arrest," Jähde waved it away. "Tell me what's going on and don't make such a mystery out of it!"

Jähde pounded his desk at every word. Willi's face closed up. If Jähde didn't believe him now either, what recourse would he have? Who could he speak to? Was it his duty to tell the story of the Jew for a second time without evidence? If his word as a Hitler Youth member wasn't trusted, he would keep quiet.

Jähde saw from Willi's face that nothing could be accomplished unless he set the boy free for an hour.

"All right," Jähde stood under the portrait of the Führer and looked Willi straight in the eye, "you're free for an hour. But don't forget what kind of responsibility you're taking on. Someone else in my position wouldn't have been so generous with you." He gave Willi his hand. "I'm counting on you!"

"I won't disappoint you, sir." Willi snapped his heels together. He wheeled abruptly and left the room.

Jähde smiled after him, half in amusement, half in satisfaction.

Jähde met Mrs. Nagold in the corridor. "Are you still packing?" he asked casually.

"I—no, of course not. My husband didn't want me to, and—" she gestured at the refugees who were still loitering in the halls, "I have responsibilities here!"

"I see," Jähde said, "your husband didn't want you to. Well, maybe he has his reasons for being so happy that the Russians are coming."

"What do you mean?" Mrs. Nagold asked, bewildered.

Jähde walked away from her without a word of explanation. She ran after him and grabbed his arm.

"What do you have against my husband?" Red spots of anxiety began to stand out on her face.

"He has a remarkable way of trivializing important things. I don't like it!"

Mrs. Nagold nodded dutifully, but Jähde was no longer paying attention. She was standing just at the spot where the young fortune-teller had read her cards. How was it again? A small dark man would bring great danger for her husband. And they should turn to a man who was a professional colleague of her husband's. He would help them.

Night had fallen. A light mist lay over the roofs of the town. The quiet of the nearby front was oppressive. Only the rolling of the tanks rumbled in the distance. Willi stood at the fountain. His new responsibility, as Jähde had put it, drove him through the town at random. He had only one wish: to find the Jew and thus to prove his sense of duty and his loyalty.

17

WHILE KIMMICH HAD GONE that afternoon to bring Abiram into safety from the town gate, Ruth had lovingly prepared things for Abiram's arrival. She set the table for three for the first time since her mother's death. Behind the granary, where the noon sun shone warmly, she picked the first violets, which she placed in a glass on the table. Suddenly her grandfather was back, alone. Without a word he took the third plate from the table.

"Where is he?"

"He ran away."

They ate supper silently and waited for darkness.

"We have to try it again," said Kimmich. "If he's still in town we have to find him. Maybe he's gone back to the town gate."

He stacked the plates thoughtfully. "If he gets hungry, maybe he will go look for food at night."

"May I come along?" Ruth asked. She had hardly spoken all evening.

"You'll have to come along, because he'll trust you!"

When Kimmich and Ruth left the house, neither of them noticed that a figure separated itself from the shadows of the granary and followed them.

Ruth thrust her hand into her grandfather's hand. They hadn't walked along hand in hand for years. Ruth had the feeling under her grandfather's protection that everything would still turn out all right.

"How quiet it is tonight," she said softly as they crossed the market square, "almost like earlier—"

"Yes," Kimmich agreed, "but it's not a good silence!"

After a while he continued more softly, "If we're lucky, the Russians will be here tomorrow. But if new Home Guard troops are sent in, then things look bad!"

"Do you know whether they'll do that?"

"No, Ruth. How should I know that? Our town is surrounded except for a little strip to the west."

Kimmich was battling a deep tiredness that had befallen him at the moment when his attempt to save the Jewish child had failed. He was oppressed not by the personal danger that linked him to Dressler through Abiram, but by suspicion and distrust.

Ruth and Kimmich came to the town gate.

"Grandfather!" Ruth said and shook Kimmich out of his thoughts. "You go up the righthand stairs, I'll go up the other side."

Ruth waited until she could hear her grandfather in the opposite tower. Suddenly she heard a rustling noise. Ruth jumped back and ran through the arch of the gate.

The noise must have come from there. A figure flitted by. Abiram! But before she could go to him, he had disappeared in the dark. The angled shadow of the gate fell far over the piles of rubble.

It would be dangerous to call out. She raised her hands to her mouth and gave the screech-owl signal. If it was Abiram, he would have to leave the shadows and come to her. Finally she saw him step cautiously away from the gray of the town wall. Ruth ran to him with outstretched hands.

"Abiram, Abiram, don't run away! It's Ruth! Grandfather and I are here to help you. Come here!" She pulled him out of the shadows into the pale moonlight.

Then she recognized Willi.

Willi laughed maliciously.

"Thank you, Ruth!"

"Willi," she screamed, but he had long since disappeared, and she stumbled sobbing back to Kimmich.

"It's my fault! I've betrayed him again and you too!"

"Who was that?"

"Willi."

"What did you tell him?"

"I didn't recognize him. I thought it was Abiram, so I called, 'Abiram, come here, Grandfather and I want to help you.' "

Kimmich nodded as if he had already known all that.

"Everyone's made mistakes, Ruth, you're not the only one."

They went back into town. Artillery began to fire in the east. The silence of the night was over.

Willi stood at attention in front of Jähde and made good his word of honor as a Hitler Youth member. He was seized by the seriousness of the moment and reported, without omitting a single detail, on the events around Abiram: his appearance, his flight, Ruth's behavior.

Jähde, who listened to Willi with growing interest, interrupted only once. "What's that you say, a Jew?"

Willi didn't tell Abiram's age. All Jews were enemies of the people, however old they were. Wasn't it better to get rid of them before they grew up and ruined the German people?

Jähde saw Willi's report as confirmation of his own suspicions of espionage. The Communist Dressler, the pacifist Kimmich, and the Jew in the Army uniform. The children had been used to carry messages so as to avoid the Gestapo. Jähde recognized the scale of this conspiracy. This was the reason that the Russian front was able to come so close to the town gates. The treason of this trio had succeeded in thwarting the use of the miracle weapon and in keeping the promised division of tanks from arriving. They had exposed the town and its people to destruction. It was now up to Jähde to save the town.

He put his hand on Willi's shoulder, and his voice was emotional.

"You have done Führer and fatherland a great service. I don't regret placing my trust in you!"

Willi's face reddened with pride. "Thank you, sir!"

"Now go. I'll see to the rest of the matter!"

At the door Jähde called him back once more.

"Not a word about this to the other boys, do you hear?"

"Yes, sir!"

"You'll answer for it if anything else goes wrong! Since you've done such a good job, I'd like to put you in charge of guarding your former friends." Jähde laughed suggestively. "I assume that you won't mind that!"

"No, sir!" Willi clicked his heels together.

Jähde went immediately to District Leader Hoffmann to convince him of the importance of this discovery. As Jähde stood outside and pressed the bell of Hoffmann's official residence in vain, he had no idea what was

192

going on behind the closed doors.

It had been a very short telephone conversation that District Leader Hoffmann had had that afternoon. Then he had passed some information to the district group leader. For hours he had burned documents in his office. Afterwards District Leader Hoffmann had begun to pack, and then he drove his official car to the warehouse and had his gas tank and reserve tank filled to the brim.

When Jähde rang, most of the work was finished and the district leader now had only to find a good moment to leave the town for the west without arousing much attention.

"What idiot can that be?" He started up as the bell racketed through the corridor.

"Just don't open it!" his wife said.

But the bell stubbornly kept ringing. Hurriedly he pulled his uniform jacket on over his civilian pants.

"Jähde, what do you want?" he asked suspiciously.

Jähde didn't notice the district leader's rudeness.

"I have to talk to you!"

He shoved his way past and into the office. Hoffmann was able to shut the door to the living room just in time. Jähde looked around the office, bewildered. Something seemed wrong, but he wasn't sure what.

"I straightened up and eliminated some old files," said the district leader, pointing to the empty shelves.

Jähde nodded and gave his report with military brevity.

"Very interesting," District Leader Hoffmann said as he feverishly thought how he could get rid of this mad chatterer.

"Do you see the connections, sir?" Jähde asked.

"Yes, yes, of course. What's his name? I mean this Jew in uniform?"

"Abiram!"

"Oh yes, I remember. He was reported as being suspected of espionage," Hoffmann said in order to distract Jähde. Hoffmann paced up and down with quick steps. This Jähde could ruin his only chance to flee. If he, Hoffmann, didn't leave the town within the next three or four hours, the way west would be cut off. What did he care about the Jew, Kimmich, or Dressler? For the district leader there was only one problem: not to fall into the hands of the Russians.

"Listen," he said suddenly, "I would like you to take over this case personally. I can't trust anyone else but you to handle this delicate affair!"

The district leader went to his desk and wrote something on a piece of paper.

"Here," he said, "that's your authorization for any-thing you need to do on the case. Use it any way you want!"

"You want to give me full authority in this case, sir?" Jähde couldn't understand why Hoffmann was giving him so much responsibility.

"Look at this assignment as evidence of your loyalty to Führer and fatherland. We're all being asked to do more today. In times of need everyone must outdo himself."

Hoffmann spoke faster and faster, he sensed that Jähde believed every word.

"Think through your procedure and report to me tomorrow. I have no more time now!"

Jähde left. In his hand he held the authorization that empowered him to do everything from arrest to court-martial, the proud crowning of his National Socialist convictions.

An insistent knocking awakened Mrs. Nagold.

"Walter," her hand felt Nagold's pillow, "listen, someone's knocking!"

Nagold woke up.

"Maybe the Russians are here," she whispered.

"My God, the Russians," he said impatiently, "why should they pick our door to knock on?"

He stood up and hopped one-legged to the door.

"I'm sorry," said Jähde roughly. He looked around the apartment. "You've unpacked again? You're not afraid any longer, is that it?"

"Did you wake me up to ask me that?"

Jähde looked Nagold up and down. He walked around the room for a long moment without saying a word to Nagold. Suddenly he stopped in front of him.

"Where is Abiram?"

Nagold, who thought he detected another phantom of Jähde's vigilance behind this question, asked: "Now who is that supposed to be, Abiram?"

"You'd better start using another tone of voice with me," said Jähde.

Nagold was startled. He was no longer dealing with a hysterical superior but with a man who was determined to go as far as he had to.

"I really can't tell you."

He suddenly noticed that standing on one leg was becoming difficult for him but didn't feel he was in the position to make himself ridiculous by hopping over to a chair in front of Jähde.

"I could almost believe you," said Jähde quietly. "If it

weren't for your sly, sneaky nature!"

With that, Jähde left the apartment.

Mrs. Nagold appeared in the doorway, her eyes wide. "What should we do," she wailed, "pack or unpack, run or stay here? They twist the meaning of everything we do!"

When Willi returned to the sleeping quarters, the boys received him with silence. They had arranged themselves in their beds so that their faces were turned toward Willi. Willi felt their contempt. Although no word of reproach had been spoken, he thought he had to defend himself. He sat on his bed and undressed.

"It's your own fault, why didn't you tell the truth!"

Willi got no answer.

"What else could I have done? Somebody had to remember that we're members of the Hitler Youth!"

No answer.

"You probably think that was easy for me. All you ever thought about was eating. Paule said it himself, his honor as a Hitler Youth member didn't go far!"

Willi listened and waited. They would have to answer sooner or later. He had undressed and stood at his bed in his pajamas.

"Is that supposed to be a punishment, that you're not speaking to me?"

He ran back and forth at the end of the beds.

Then he stopped in front of Antek.

"All right, I'm sworn to silence, but since we were friends once, I'll tell you the truth."

But there was no question, no head was raised, nothing.

Willi stood in front of Antek's bed.

"Jähde learned about the connections only indirectly through me. It was your friend Ruth who put me on the right track."

Willi hoped that Antek would defend Ruth.

But there was nothing.

Willi lost his nerve. He jumped onto Antek's bed. "Just you listen! It was your Ruth, with her war traitor grandfather!"

Antek's only answer was to turn over.

Willi jumped down from the bed. "That's how you want to get me? It won't work. Not with me! I have orders from Jähde to guard you!"

Beside himself with rage, Willi tore his straw mat from the bed and threw it down at an angle in front of the door.

"As long as I'm lying in front of the door, none of you gets out."

He locked the door, wrapped himself in his blanket, and kept the key in his hand. "You deserve this, and it serves you right."

The first rays of morning broke through the blackout paper. Zick woke up. He saw Willi lying diagonally in front of the door. Paule and Antek were fast asleep. Zick thought things over. He had to go to the bathroom. But how was he supposed to get out the door without speaking to Willi? Before Willi had come back yesterday, they had promised each other not to speak to him. Zick felt for his slippers cautiously. Willi woke up immediately.

"Where do you think you're going?" he growled.

"To the bathroom!" Zick hissed back furiously, hoping that Antek and Paule would not count that as a breach of promise.

Willi seemed undecided. Perhaps this was a trap.
Zick shifted from one leg to the other.

"Pig," Willi muttered angrily and opened the door, "you'll be sorry if you're not back in ten minutes!"

He grabbed Zick by the pajama collar. "I'll be watching from the window, friend, so don't do anything stupid."

Zick disappeared in the dawn light of the corridor.

The upstairs toilets were locked. Zick went down one flight. The blue night light was shining in the corridors here. Zick clambered over sacks and suitcases. People were sleeping in the hall. Everyone had an arm wrapped tightly around their possessions. Zick was relieved to find a door free on the lower floor. He slid quietly along the wall to avoid waking anyone.

Then one of the classroom doors opened and a slight figure rushed out. Abiram. Zick recognized him immediately. Then Abiram saw Zick, too, and moved cautiously toward him. "You can't leave," Zick whispered. "Willi's watching at the window. They're after you!"

"Does anyone know I'm here?"

"Maybe."

"Is there another way out?" Abiram asked. He looked out the window at the sky, which was getting lighter by the minute. "Is there someplace to hide here?"

Zick took him by the hand. They walked through the long corridor without haste, so that no one could have thought they were anything but two students from the boarding school going to their sleeping quarters.

They climbed the stairs to the next floor. They had passed Nagold's apartment and had reached the topmost step.

"In there," Zick said into Abiram's ear. He pointed to a door without a handle. "The attic. You have to keep all the way to the left, otherwise the Nagolds will be able to hear you. At the end there are a couple of steps down. You can hide there under the eaves between the rafters."

"And no one goes up there?"

"No. Now that there's shooting, no one uses the attic."

Zick was about to turn around when Abiram held him back.

"Will you come back?"

"Yes, we'll come. I'll wake Antek up. He'll know what to do. You don't need to be afraid!"

Zick leaned on the banister and slid downstairs as Abiram disappeared into the attic.

Willi had slept for a few minutes despite Zick's absence. When Zick carefully stepped over him, he just waved as a sign that he had taken note of Zick's return. Then he turned onto his side. His round face lay with half-opened lips on the pillow. He was asleep.

Zick crept out of his bed and slipped under the blanket with Antek. Antek awoke immediately. Breathlessly Zick whispered to him that he had met Abiram and had hidden him in the attic.

Willi didn't awaken when Antek got Paule up, and he didn't awaken as the three boys got dressed. Even when the lace to Paule's boot broke and his elbow hit with a muffled sound against the edge of the bed, Willi only grunted.

Antek nudged Paule. Who should be the first to try to step over Willi? Paule showed Antek his fist, then pointed to Willi's chin. Antek knelt beside Willi. If

Willi woke up, Antek would send him back to sleep with a punch to the jaw. Now Paule was stepping over Willi, and the only sound was the boys' breathing. It went very quickly. Antek shut the door behind him, as the last one out.

They hurried to the attic. After a short search they discovered Abiram. They didn't shake his hand, they didn't even greet him. They sat down next to him on the rafters.

"Tell us how you got here."

Abiram told them.

"That was Kimmich," Antek said when Abiram told about the man with the white hair who knew his name.

"Then Ruth told after all," Paule said.

"Maybe Willi threatened her," Antek answered.

"Maybe!"

Antek rolled a dustball between his fingers. "Kimmich was our last hope," he said and rolled the little ball down the angle of a rafter.

"But he's in danger himself," Paule said.

Abiram nodded.

"I can think of one other possibility," Antek said slowly.

"What?"

Zick scooted closer.

"I'll go to Nagold!"

Paule made a negative gesture. "He—"

"I've always liked him. He'll help if I go to him."

"But you know how he acted when we were late that time," Paule protested.

"That was another matter. We didn't trust him, and so he got angry."

"And if that doesn't work?" Zick whispered.

"He's right," Abiram said, "what Antek is planning is dangerous."

Antek didn't want to listen to his friends.

"I'll go to him before everyone wakes up. You stay up here. Nobody leave the attic until I come back!"

He didn't wait for their agreement but started off right away. The others stayed back between the rafters and the roof with their hearts pounding.

Antek had thought through what he wanted to do. The best thing would be to take Nagold to the attic and present him with the accomplished fact. Antek believed he could somehow help them in this dangerous situation.

"Has something happened, Antek?" Nagold asked uneasily as Antek stood at his door in agitation.

"Yes, Mr. Nagold. It has to do with our being late for choir practice and with Dressler. Will you help us?"

Nagold sensed the danger in Antek's question. He resisted with all the strength he had. What did they want from him? Hadn't he done enough? And what did the Communist Dressler have to do with him?

Finally Nagold said, "What do you want?"

"I'd like you to come with me."

Nagold held tight to the latch. He felt like slamming the door in the boy's face. All this was none of his business.

Antek turned around. "Will you come?"

Without further questions Nagold limped up the stairs behind Antek, across the dusty, empty attic floor to the cranny among the beams where he found Paule, Zick, and a strange dark-haired boy. They were all watching him.

"Who is this?" Nagold asked.

He had expected to find Dressler here.

Antek went to stand beside Abiram.

"He's a refugee. We found him in our cellar. He doesn't have any parents."

"Then he's got to go to an assembly point just like everyone else. Is that any reason to hide him up here in the attic?"

"No," Antek answered slowly, "but we have to hide him because Jähde and Willi are after him."

Nagold understood less and less, and he felt himself becoming angry. "You're exaggerating, children. Why should Mr. Jähde and Willi, of all people, be after a refugee boy?"

The boys exchanged glances. Abiram shrank against the rafters. Now they would have to say it. Antek reached into his pocket. Without saying a word, he handed Nagold the star of David.

"Is his name Abiram?" Nagold asked, his gaze on Antek's hand.

"Yes," Antek said, "and Willi knows him. He told Jähde everything. Kimmich wanted to help Abiram, but Abiram ran away because he was afraid of him."

"I see," Nagold interrupted quickly, "Kimmich wanted to help. Why didn't you go to him, then? He knows much better what to do in situations like this. Why did you come to me? What can I do?" Nagold spoke quickly. "Kimmich is the better man for your escape plans!"

"We can't get out of here without you," Antek said. "We need you and we're depending on you. Kimmich can only help us once we've gotten Abiram out of the school!"

Nagold turned around. Had he been crippled for

Führer and fatherland only in order to die for a Jewish boy? If Jähde found out he was behind this, he knew he would be courtmartialed.

"What's the link between your Abiram and Dressler?"

Antek told him.

"Do you know that Dressler is a Communist with a warrant out against him?"

"That doesn't matter now," answered Paule.

"It doesn't matter? No, my boy, you're wrong. Jähde suspects that Dressler, Kimmich, and Abiram are spies!"

"But we've got to get out of here, or he's lost. Don't you understand that?"

Antek felt Nagold's hesitation.

"Yes, I understand." Nagold suddenly knew that the best thing was to do nothing.

"I've seen and heard nothing. Maybe that will help the Jew. And you," he looked at Antek and Paule, "see to it that you get back to your sleeping quarters as fast as possible."

Nagold didn't look around, didn't ask whether the boys would follow his advice, and he didn't care how the Jew was to get out of there. He dragged himself through the dust toward the exit. The boys were alone. "Well," said Abiram and tried to smile. "Then I'll just go."

"Where will you go?"

"I don't know, Antek. It doesn't much matter where you get caught. I'm a Jew, after all. I'd forgotten it, being around you."

He extended his hand to Antek.

"Farewell!"

Antek ignored his hand. "You're not going!"

"Yes I am."

"Then we're coming with you!" Paule said suddenly.

"No, Paule. I'm a Jew. You just turn Jews loose, that's what your teacher said."

Antek slapped the dust from his pants.

"We're not going to leave Abiram alone, he's one of us!"

They crept out of their hiding place, took Abiram into the middle, walked across the attic floor and pushed the door open. They climbed down the stairs to the front door of the boarding school, looked neither right nor left, and paid no attention to who might be watching them or following them.

18

MRS. NAGOLD, AGITATED, circled around her husband, who was on a stool in the kitchen with his artificial leg stretched out in front of him.

"A Jew in the building!" she sobbed in fear. "That's as good as a death sentence!"

"The boys were hoping that I would get their Jew to safety," Nagold said.

Mrs. Nagold knelt in front of him. "Jähde asked about this Abiram yesterday, didn't he?"

"Yes, he suspected me."

Her hand clasped him. "That means . . ."

Nagold nodded.

"You've got to report the Jew!" she whispered.

"He's a child!"

"Oh, a child," Mrs. Nagold said, leaping up. "Did we make the laws we have to live with?"

Nagold didn't move.

Mrs. Nagold yelled at her husband, "Say something. You just sit there as if all this had nothing to do with you!" Fear was making her angry. "Something's got to be done, or do you want to wait until Mr. Jähde is ready to arrest you?"

She shouted into his face and shook him by the lapels.

"Listen," she said suddenly very quietly, "does this Jew have black hair?"

"Yes."

"And is he small?"

She nodded before he could answer. Now she knew. This Jew was the little man who would bring her husband bad luck, and now she had to seek help from a man who had a professional connection with her husband. Of course, she had to see Jähde in order to save her husband.

"Why do you ask?" Nagold wondered, puzzled.

"I don't know," she said. "I'll be right back, I have to go down to the kitchen."

He was glad when she left the room.

A rumor had torn the refugees out of their sleep. The road west was said to be cut off. The Russians had supposedly surrounded the town and no one could leave. The first wagons that had set out that morning were said to be on their way back.

Mrs. Nagold heard none of that. She ran to Jähde. He hadn't been to bed. His desk was littered with sheets of paper covered with the penciled names of Dressler, Kimmich, and Abiram, over and over.

"Mr. Jähde," Mrs. Nagold panted, "my husband is innocent! Believe me!"

"Speak up!"

"There's a Jew in the attic! Antek and Paule hid him there. They wanted my husband to smuggle him out."

Jähde was already at the door.

"So it was true!" he shouted.

"But he didn't do it! He didn't do it! Can't you hear me?"

Mrs. Nagold stumbled after Jähde. "He didn't do it! He didn't do it!" Her legs gave out. She pulled herself up along the banister. "He didn't do it! Listen to me!"

Someone uncurled her fingers from the banister. "Calm down, for God's sake!"

She pressed the strange hands. "He really didn't do it," she murmured and only then saw that it wasn't Jähde next to her, but a refugee.

As he ran by, Jähde pushed the door of the boys' sleeping quarters open. Willi was shoved ungently across the floor.

"Come out of there right now if you care what happens to you!"

Willi tumbled out of his slumber. The other boys' beds were empty and their things were gone.

As Jähde reached the top of the stairs, he saw Nagold coming toward him.

"Get those boys down here!" Jähde shouted and waved his pistol.

Nagold limped up the last few steps to the attic.

Jähde's curses followed him. He was glad to reach the dusty emptiness of the attic.

"Antek!"

Nagold ran to the other end of the attic. "Antek, Paule!"

He climbed through the beams. He called and shouted. He pleaded for the boys to come out of their hiding places, until he realized that he was all alone up there.

Nagold held onto a rafter.

"They're gone," he whispered. The boys had taken

the risk of saving a Jew. Nagold felt miserably ashamed of himself. He wasn't just a cripple—the rafters started to dance before his eyes. He fell down, and his hands grasped air. Next to him the attic window shattered.

The bombardment had started. The first hit was the gasoline depot on the grounds of the little factory. Nagold pulled himself up. The boys must be wandering around the town senseless with fear. He had to get them into a cellar.

Willi saw Nagold push Jähde aside and descend the stairs in a strange hopping manner.

"They're gone!" Nagold pushed his wife aside. "Get into the crypt."

He shook her off.

"I don't want to!" She hung on him. "I'd rather die with you."

She clutched his clothes and wouldn't let him go.

He pulled her hands away by force. "Take my wife to the shelter," he told a young woman and then disappeared in the turmoil.

Willi was alone with Jähde.

The sirens screamed and the bells thundered.

"Nothing is lost yet!" Willi shouted into Jähde's pale face. I'll bring you the Jew! I promise you!"

Jähde didn't hear. He ran to the window and saw the market square filling with people who were hurrying toward the church in order to take shelter in the crypt.

The first machine-gun fire cracked at the edge of town. Jähde knew what that meant. The Russians were at the gates of the town.

Jähde's hand felt for his authorization. The Jew had escaped. What should he report to the district leader? Should he tell him the Jew had completed his work of treason under the roof of the boarding school with his own students?

"Bring me the Jew!" he roared at Willi. "Go on, bring him here!" His fingers cramped around the authorization.

The upper floors of the boarding school had emptied out. While Willi hurried down the stairs to find Abiram, Jähde ran from door to door upstairs.

"Give me the Jew, the swine!" he yelled.

The old granary had received a direct hit. The steeply sloping roof bowed inward as if crushed by a giant hand. Yellowish-gray clouds of dirt rolled over the market square.

Willi rubbed his eyes. He was coughing so much he could hardly draw breath. He felt his way forward, trying to get to the crypt. That's where the boys must be with Abiram. Willi stumbled, fell, and cut his face open. I have to find him, he thought, I promised!

At the side street that led to the church square, he saw Antek and Ruth. The Jew couldn't be far away. He caught up with the two of them. People were crowding in front of the church. Kimmich saw Willi appear behind Ruth and Antek.

"Did you go and get him?" Kimmich asked.

"Who?"

Only now did Antek see Willi standing behind him.

"No," Antek shook his head, "I'd never go and get him. Let him take care of himself!"

Kimmich didn't listen to Antek's answer. He wanted to take Willi along into the crypt.

"Come on, boy," he said.

But Willi evaded him as if contact with the old man repelled him. "Where is Abiram?" he screamed.

More and more people were pressing around them. It was all Willi could do not to be pulled along into the church.

"He's with me!" Kimmich yelled back. The shooting had begun again. "Be reasonable and come on into the cellar!"

Willi rowed with his arms to defend himself against the stream of people. He would never hide in the church while Jähde was waiting for his report. He had to get back so Jähde could get the Jew and Kimmich out of the crypt.

Bullets whipped across the street. Somewhere men were screaming. Some soldiers jumped through the cellar windows of a building. Willi crawled out from under an overturned wagon where he had taken shelter. He ran down the street bent over, as he had seen the soldiers doing.

Suddenly someone grabbed and held him. He was looking into the bearded face of an old man in civilian clothing. He had a rifle in his hand and a band with a swastika around his arm. He was a member of the Home Guard.

"Where are you going, boy?"

"To make a report!"

"To the Russians?"

Willi hit the old man in the stomach, and he released him, cursing.

Now all Willi had to do was cross the market square. Suddenly he was afraid. The square had never seemed so large as now. Maybe he should hide in a cellar too. Willi clenched his fists and crawled on all fours across the square. A searing pain shot into his back; it spread through his whole body and then disappeared. There was a strange silence around Willi. He didn't understand why he could see shots landing all around him but couldn't hear them.

He saw Jähde come out of the school, getting bigger and bigger. The rifle shots bounced off his chest like balls, and his brown uniform boots shone like a thousand suns. "The Jew is in the crypt," Willi said. He felt but couldn't hear himself talk.

Jähde came out of the building carrying his pistol. There were dead men and women lying in the streets who had been unable to reach the cellar in time. A child was crying somewhere among the shots and the explosions of grenades. Nagold came running across the square from the direction of the granary. His face was covered with dirt. He waved. Jähde wondered whether Nagold had finally decided to do his duty as a National Socialist.

"Did you get rid of the Jew?"

Nagold looked at Jähde as if he had lost his mind.

"Willi is dead!" said Nagold.

Jähde didn't respond.

"Willi is dead!" Nagold repeated.

Jähde whirled around, enraged. "Is that my fault? What are you doing here, anyway?"

"I was looking for the children."

"Well," Jähde asked sarcastically, "did you find them?"

"Yes, Kimmich took them into the crypt. The Jew too."

"What?" Jähde raised his pistol.

Nagold was quicker. The weapon flew in a high arch over both of their heads, onto the street.

A couple of Home Guard members were creeping

along the row of buildings opposite. They were carrying a white flag.

"Are you crazy?" Jähde bellowed. Paying no attention to the shots, he ran across the street. "No surrender! I forbid it! I have full authorization!"

"From whom?"

"From District Leader Hoffmann! The town isn't to surrender!"

"That's who gave you an authorization? You can wipe your ass with it, if you still . . ."

The men laughed.

"Your district leader, man," one of them said and tapped a finger against his forehead, "he took off last night with bag and baggage. They say he was one of the last to get through!"

"He took off?" stammered Jähde. He couldn't grasp it.

The men left him standing there with Nagold.

"Over there," Nagold said, and pointed to the place, "there's Willi. He's dead, and it's your fault!"

Jähde didn't answer. If he wanted to save his life, his only chance was to win Nagold over. "Yes, my friend," Jähde began with a frozen smile on his face, "you're probably right."

When Nagold didn't answer, he continued. "But I was able to see that only because of your initiative. I was wrong about you. If someone like you had been our district leader, this war would have ended differently!"

Nagold stared at Jähde. An hour ago this man had wanted to shoot him, had demanded the death of a Jewish child, and now he was speaking in praise and recognition.

He turned around without a word, Jähde at his side.

"Did you actually know this Jew?"

"Yes. He's a child!"

"What, he's a child? And you didn't tell me that?" Jähde was dismayed.

"Then I've committed a terrible error! My dear Nagold," he said softly, "I assume that you will have some understanding for your former superior. After all, I didn't turn you in."

He looked cautiously at Nagold.

"And do we want to announce, too," Nagold shouted, "that Willi's death was a just punishment on the part of fate? That this child was persecuting a Jew without any orders, with no model for it, just because he had a warped nature?"

"Now, now, Nagold, don't get excited. Willi was a hot-head who took things too seriously. I'm sorry about it, but he just wasn't made of the right stuff!"

In the crypt fear had grown into the torments of hell. Every nook was full. People were sitting almost on top of each other. Mortar crumbled down from the cracked walls. The wide pillars that supported the vault trembled under the shock of the detonations. People had shoved the altar to the Virgin Mary up against the wall. On its steps, with their backs to the statue of the Virgin, sat the four boys, Ruth, and Kimmich. The darkness increased the fear and uncertainty. No one was ashamed of being afraid. People recited prayers aloud, sobbed, wailed, lamented, accused. Impatience alternated with resignation, malice with kindness. "Stop that praying," cried a voice behind the altar, "God has no time for us!"

Finally the door was pulled open. Nagold limped

down the steps. He saw Abiram, the boys, and Kimmich.

"The Russians are here!" he said.

No one moved. They all sat there in numb horror, unable to judge whether this news was good or bad.

Kimmich got up. He was first to go to the open door. Abiram and Ruth followed him, and Antek, Paule, and Zick came after.

"Do we have peace now?" asked Mrs. Nagold quietly. She didn't dare look her husband in the eye.

"Yes, peace," he said. He leaned on her shoulder as she walked with him to the door.

LEONIE OSSOWSKI was born in 1925 in Silesia, once a German province but now part of Poland. Like all Germans living in Silesia at the end of World War II, she and her family were forced to leave their homes. Ms. Ossowski was 19 when they moved. Her family moved to Thuringia, which soon after became part of East Germany. She now lives in West Berlin.

In addition to *Star without a Sky,* Leonie Ossowski's work includes other novels, short stories, plays, and films. *Star without a Sky* has been published in both East Germany and West Germany as well as in Denmark, Sweden, and Holland.